> *I love all waste*
> *And solitary places; where we taste*
> *The pleasure of believing what we see*
> *Is boundless, as we wish our souls to be:*

BYRON

# Contents

# AUTHOR'S NOTE

In this parallel Italy, some names are spelled phonetically. But an <u>e</u> at the end of a name is always sounded, (as <u>ay</u> to rhyme with <u>day</u>.)

PART ONE

# The Mask

# 1

"I SPIT ON THE VIRGIN. She's a whore."

The shadow of the bridge, ghostly in the pre-dawn, closed them over. And Furian thought quickly. *How wonderful life is.*

Then the shadow lifted. They were out on the canal, and the wanderlier was crossing himself. "Forgive me, Beautiful Maria."

Furian thought, *Am I so superstitious then. I must do it too? Tell myself a lie, like this man's extreme piety.* (For sometimes they only said, My wife's faithless, or I long to be impotent.)

But the Bridge of Liars, crossing or riding under which you must always lie for good luck, was gone.

Only the canal now, leaden pearl under a half-born sky.

"I don't think you will find anyone, Signore." said the wanderlier.

"No. You're right. It's unusual."

"My cousin, Chomo, he found two yesterday by the water steps at Santa Lala. A girl and a man. Lovers, perhaps.

"I should have hired you then."

"This was in broad morning, Signore. They were

*13*

caught together by her hair. She had very long hair. Pale yellow. It was a shame."

Furian thought, *Shaachen would have liked that*. But he only said, "Never mind. We'll go towards the Primo. You can get another fare there easily."

"Thank you, Signore. You're always considerate."

*Oh yes*, thought Furian. *Always, always*.

The canal turned, and they came out into wider water. On either side, the dim, dark houses rose, peeling like dying flowers. Iron balconies hung over their heads like the empty cages of enormous birds. A lamp burned, one solitary pink ember.

The wanderlier sang mournfully some kind of sad song:

*"And so farewell; laugh when you think of me,*
*"Who loved you better, better, better:*
*"He will make you weep—"*

The voice of the wanderlier was muffled by the mask he wore, a cheap concoction of paste and board, the shape of a fish's face.

Furian was tired. He longed to sleep, and knew he would not do so, to attempt it would be foolish. Behind his own mask, that of a plain, grotesque white face with a long, pointing nose, he closed his eyes.

The lamp shone on his lids as they passed beneath. And like the Bridge of Lies, was gone.

It had been a fruitless night, from three o'clock searching the canals and pools of the island City for dead bodies to give to Doctor Shaachen. During the autumn carnival, there were often dead, usually murder victims, sometimes not even out in the water, let alone weighted down. Last year Furian had taken five in a night, one a young gallant who had been hanged from a lamp-standard, only his beautiful silver buckled shoes tip-toeing in the canal. The wanderlier yawned.

"My wife will be frying little blue fish," he said, "baking bread. But not," he added, "for me."

Furian grunted.

"Oh, Signore," said the boatman, guiding his wanderer, dark and slick as a dagger between two bulging leaning house fronts, "my wife hates me. She's in love with our son. He's at the University, you understand."

Furian said, softly, "I'm sorry."

"No, I don't mean," said the boatman, as if Furian had asked or insisted, "that she's incestuous. Only that her love is fresh for him. For me, burned out. And when I go home, she says to me, Look at you, Juseppi, you have the face of a fish."

Furian felt he must stir himself. "What does she wear for Carnival?"

"A mask like a dove, with black-ringed eyes. And she wears a white gown. The tops of her breasts are still soft and white, with marbled blue veins. When I touch, she says, Go away, you fish."

"Change your mask," said Furian.

"Last year I was a bull. She told me then she was afraid of me. She made me sleep in my boat."

Furian laughed. He said, "Forgive me. Why don't you take a mistress?"

"Yes. I'll do it. I'll make an offering at the Primo. The first girl I see. Thank you, Signore."

There was a faintly lighted window above, either a late window or an early one. The lattice cast a reflection on the water like black lace.

Just beyond, the waterway closed in again, a channel hardly wide enough even for the narrow wandering boat. But the sky was higher, a ceiling of whitish nacre, and something floated on the water like a blown blossom.

"What's that—look, Signore—a face in the canal."

Furian had got up, careful of the rhythm of the boat. Juseppi the wanderlier poked them forward with his oar, and firmed them in, piercing with the oar the sludge of mud and filth and history under the boat.

The wanderer stood trembling-still.

The water was black as ink here, rimmed with ripples like silver milk. The face floated, upturned, as Furian had seen many faces in this half light, at this season. Was it weed or black hair that wavered out behind? The dead eyes staring at the dawn, so far above, so useless to them.

"In God's name—" said Furian, surprising himself. He felt dizzy a moment, and the movement of his long hair, tied back at the nape of his neck, slipping forward over his shoulder—was like a serpent's touch on his skin.

"It's a *mask*, Signore."

"So it is."

"But it's been in a fight."

"Yes."

"Shall I search about—something may be down there."

Furian sat. "If it's down that deep, he won't want it."

For Shaachen did not care for the weighted ones, he liked them salad crisp, their lungs with only a little salty water in them.

But the mask was strange. It seemed to have been ripped and bruised. Yes, bruised, as if made of flesh. Skeins of black hair eddied back from it, but they were torn and ragged. About the eye-holes were scales of brassy sequins, but some had come off. One lay neatly on the water like a dull yellow tear.

The mask had been only half-face, resembling a sculpture, some god or handsome classical figure, a perfect nose, and chiseled brows, painted black—for a moment it looked familiar.

All across the right side was a slash, an old rusty color, as if the mask—had bled.

There was something very odd, very sinister in its appearance. But it was the sleepless nights, wine and brandy, the rocking of the boat, which made it nauseous and terrible.

Furian decided. "Use your hook. Bring it in."

"Signore—you want it?"

"Yes. We found nothing else. Let him have that."

The wanderlier gripped his hook, and reached for the mask. As he secured it, the oar let go of the mud and they drifted on.

Furian felt a spasm of distaste as the bruised white mask fluttered heavily off into the boat. It's dead hair spread over his foot.

The boatman crossed himself again.

"He's down below us."

"Perhaps. Or he went home with a bloody nose."

"Without the mask?"

To be unmasked at Carnival was, by the law of misrule, illegal. At least, you would be hounded, fined, even if you were rich, or holy.

"Well. Let's row for the Primo."

The wanderlier turned his wanderer through the narrow way, between arches, where three blind lamps hung down and the dawn shone in them, like mother-of-pearl.

Quickly they came out into a lagoon, the Laguna Fulvia.

The water was a sheet of lilac ice, and from it ascended wan palaces that seemed already drowned. So still was everything a moment, the reflections of the walls of Venus, City of the Sea, appeared more solid and more real than her vaporous buildings floating in twilight above.

Furian noted, as if he must, the huge white dome of the Primo Suvio, and beyond, the transparent veiled amber minarets of the Palace of Justice and the Temple of Art. But the sun was rising, yet one more gilded dome.

Furian shut his eyes. Damn beauty. He would give it all to the ocean for three hours of sleep. Or no. He would die for it, the longest sleep of all.


THERE WAS NO NEED to disguise the find inadequately as a carpet, or something in a chest. Furian went alone, by the route of the alleys, to Shaachen's house.

To the south, steps led into the water, and there was an imposing pole to moor a boat, topped by a green iron Neptune. On the alley front, the palace looked mean, its windows narrow, sides stained, and scrawled by occasional graffiti. The narrow door, almost always open by day, led into the lower rooms, where Doctor Shaachen's free clinic was, as usual, full of destitutes and criminals. Drinking, smoking of pipes, and a card game were in progress. Elsewhere sat the desperate, jittery or slumped patrons. They would lurk here all day for the Doctor, ready to present their various ailments and diseases. Some he would cure, some, it was said, he killed. He was reckoned very clever, but would always say, (they said), Now, this medicine hasn't yet been tested. It may make you well, or worse. May do nothing. May even harm you. Go home, take it, come back in seven days and tell me what's happened to you. (And, they said, sometimes even the dead had done so.)

Ignoring the patients, who mostly ignored him in turn, Furian climbed the stair, walked the corridor, and rapped on a black door.

"Devil take you. Devil blast you, I say," Shaachen cried. "What do you want?"

"Nothing," said Furian. "Good morning and farewell."

He waited, and the door was flung open.

"Furian. Shit of stars. You have something? In that bag? A *head*? Come in."

Furian shrugged, and entered Doctor Shaachen's study.

The window faced to the south, across the canal, but it was filled by small squares of opaque, greenish glass. Against it stood a painterly array of bottles, liquid apricot, jade, and powdery mauve—an effect of pleasing color that was quite random. The fine orrery and astrolabe had been pushed aside, the old books jostled on shelves. Distillers' glasses stood on the table, crowded by the ancient stuffed turtle with a shell of agate. Papers littered the floor. Spider webs massed from the ceiling. The room smelled of stagnant brews, brandy, the canal outside, and of Shaachen's pet magpie, which was standing on the turtle's back, eating some raw shreds of meat out of its dish.

"So, Furian Furiano. Show me."

"It isn't what you think."

"Not a head? A leg, then? A *child*—?"

Shaachen experimented on fresh corpses. He found them handy. The City police did not hamper him, being well-bribed.

Shaachen leaned forward. He had on, as was nor-

mal, his black wig of long curls, under which he was
shaved bald. Indoors, he went unmasked, and his face,
like the black magpie's face, was that of a wicked old
woman. Here and there in the alleys they said that he
was truly two hundred years old, having sold his soul to
Lucefero for knowledge. Probably he was sixty.

"You'll be disappointed," said Furian.

"That's," said Shaachen nastily, "what you say to all
the girls."

Furian said, "It's not flesh. I couldn't find you any
flesh to eat or feed to your bird. But I thought it might
interest you."

"Give me," said Shaachen. "On the table there."

Furian emptied the bag over the small space on the
table. The mask fell out and lay there. Shaachen's magpie flew up with a croak and blue flash from its black and
white feathers.

"A mask. At Carnival he brings me a mask!"

Furian said, "If it's of no concern to you, I'll take it
back—"

"Wait, wait. Where did you find this?"

"In the water. A street near Fulvia."

"Nothing else."

"Nothing I could see."

Shaachen peered at the mask through a magnifying
glass. He touched it, but with a rod, a pair of tongs.

"Something strange. Something peculiar. I look,
and expect his eyes to look back at me out of the holes.
And perhaps, the reflection of his assassin in them. And
perhaps they will. No, I forgive you, Furian Furiano.
Something, some thing. I'll give you the price of a full-
grown hand. How's that?"

"Very generous."

As Shaachen was unlocking his chest, he said, slyly,

"In two nights, there'll be a Revel of Diana. At the full moon." Furian waited once more. "Do you want the work? Bring a companion with you. Only one should be needed. But a hefty fellow."

"I can arrange that."

"We won't meet here, but by the Centurion's Bridge. The Neptune side. Eleven, by the Primo clock."

There came a scratch at the door. Shaachen called in a more friendly voice. A well-dressed woman came in with a tray. She had the mask of a pigeon, and Furian thought of Juseppi the boatman, and his marble-breasted wife. Dull-brazen hair threaded with grey ran down this one's back. Shaachen had cured her of a growth, (he had said, by painting his member with a certain remedy and having intercourse with her.) Now she brought him breakfast every day. There was a whole roast chicken, warm bread under a napkin, peaches. She set down the tray on the space from which Shaachen had, with the tongs, suddenly whipped away the mask.

The chicken was aromatic. Furian felt a hollow pang of hunger.

"Eat with me," said Doctor Shaachen.

"Thank you, no."

Furian picked up the coins. As he was leaving, the woman was slicing a peach into a cup of wine, and the smell of nectar filled the air. The magpie had come down again and Shaachen, calling it "Darling," was feeding portions of chicken to its black beak.

THE CITY OF THE SEA, commonly called Venus, although her name been had Venera, stood—or drifted, in the popular view—on her seven islands. She was aproned by the three great lagoons which held her, Fulvia, Aquila,

Silvia, and all through her ran her canals, cutting her in delicate pieces. Seen high from the air, as the sable gulls of the ocean saw her, she was like a broken mirror, reflecting sky. The broken, attributable mirror of course, of Venus.

In the market beyond Shaachen's palazzo, the early vegetables and fruit and fronded herbs were lying in sheets of color, that swam momentarily before Furian's eyes. He could have bitten into everything, the melons, the curled basil, (green, succulent), the purple legumes, the bosoms of young women bending, creamy, to their baskets, where just a slip, a shiver, and the whole breast, a globe of heaven, might be, for half a second, revealed. The inside of his mouth was wet, and he was suddenly hard under his clothes.

For this reason, he would wait. No breakfast. No woman.

He looked instead at the masks of the poor, antiques passed down through generations, kept sacred with the little Virgin statue, the medallion of Neptune, mended, patched. Sometimes only a band of black cloth with two eyeholes cut out. The beggars who clustered at the market's edge sported masks of straw or dead leaves. One had omitted the custom last year, and been hung up barefaced by the heels among the wrung-neck chickens.

Six weeks the autumn Carnival lasted. They were one week into it. He had missed the first five days, lying down with fever in his rat's nest. He must go to the rat's nest now, tidy the mess. Then to the Signora's, to copy her book for her.

A box-litter passed along the market's rim. Four men in ivory livery, holding up a doll in a wonderful mask. It was the shape they especially liked this year, that of an opened fan, narrow end at the chin, all silver lace

done in white and black, with brazen sequins about the eyes. It was one of the finest masks to be had, modeled on the Apollo at Aquila—"

Furian said, courteously, "And was the young man known to you?"

"Only by word of mouth, Signore Furian. A lovely example of youth, which all too often now, disappoints."

After this exchange, the Signora became exhausted early—it was only four. She went away and left him to his copying. And on the stroke of six the maid came in and told him he must go.

It was as he was walking down the steps to the waiting boat, getting into it, feeling the familiar rhythm of the water, which seemed to rock all Ve-Nera-Venus, that he saw, in his inner vision, the slashed mask floating upon the twilight canal.

Yes, it had been modeled upon a classic Apollo. Yes, it was a half-mask, ending at the upper lip. It was white with black, and sequined. It was, of its kind, impressive.

That then the victim who lay under the water—if he did—Cloudio del Nero.

Would it be worth while telling Shaachen? Having the canal dragged. Someone might pay to have up the corpse.

But Furian found this disgusting. To hunt for corpses for scientific Shaachen's pittance, yes perhaps. But to crawl to some great house, to make a pimp of oneself for death, To wrest away money (I know *where*), and feed off grief. To become for those Great Ones what they expected: rubbish. And Shaachen anyway had no care for cash. He had plenty, it would seem. And the corpse would by now be far too drowned to take his tinctures and sewings.

Let it lie.

# 2

THE BLISSFUL MELODY WOKE HIM, but before he woke, he thought of heaven, so perfect, so unknown it was.

Then, coming up from the comfortless doze, he identified a coarse voice singing in the street, the tune distorted, lost—for a second it had sounded like an angel, not a drunk.

New songs came and went like days in Venus. They were sung to death, in rooms, in alleys, on the canals. Until this evening, it had been that dirge the boatman—Juseppi?—had maundered out—Oh I loved you better, better.

Now it would be this one.

Furian shook himself. He had fallen asleep for ten or twenty minutes in his straight chair. From the wine, probably.

There had been a time he enjoyed drinking, and had kept to abstemious drinking customs. Now he hated the taste of it—vinegar, wormwood—He poured another glass.

But the glass itself was fair. The smoky greenness of it, like some cleaner water in winter.

That song, it rang on in his head. No words, but

the luminous melody, so slow; a largo. Even warbled by a drunk.

The clock struck from the church of Santa Lala across the lagoon. It was ten, here, and not much more by the Primo, for all clocks told different times. The sun was gone three hours. Oh God, the pointless melancholy of night.

Furian put on his coat—the mask stayed fixed to his face, its parted lips still moist from the wine.

He went out, and down the sixty seven stairs. He had had his sleep, all twenty-three minutes of it, and would get no more. He would go instead about the City, and later maybe again search for corpses for Shaachen. He would need to find a ruffian, too, for the Revel of Diana.

IT WAS TRUE. They were playing the song about the City. He heard snatches of it—unintelligibly at the drinking shop two streets from his apartment, on the Silvia Lagoon, as he was rowed towards Santa Lala—a passing boat with lamplit cabin, where thin high voices fluted and chimed.

"That's a nice song," said the wanderlier who rowed him. "I'll learn it tomorrow. It's about love, don't you think."

"I would guess so," said Furian.

The boatman was masked as a water-rat. Did his wife fear him? Make him sleep in the boat?

As he walked through the byways towards Aquila, revelers passed Furian. They were masked as gods and goddesses, nymphs and satyrs. Not only faces, but wigs and bizarre clothes, horns. Their rustic garments were of silk, and men with torches and clubs escorted them.

Furian stopped to drink at a bar that spread along the arches by the Equus Gardens, and here he heard again the song, and some of the words. They seemed strange. But the melody was piercing-sweet, like pain. A man came by, selling song-sheets.

"I'll take one."

Furian gave him a bronze ducca, and the man said, "The last *he'll* write."

"Who?"

"Some dead man."

"A dead man wrote this?"

"Dead now."

The seller shambled on and Furian scanned the sheet. It was badly written and eccentrically spelled. Very likely it was inaccurate. But the song seemed to have a story. A princess who would not smile. Her lovers must win her by bringing an expression of happiness to her face. None could do it.

It was some old tale, transposed for music. Furian seemed to recall it—surely the lovers, or suitors, had been beheaded or hanged when their efforts failed. And indeed, the last line read, or seemed to: *And he can only die*. As had the composer, presumably.

Something moved in the canal-depths of Furian's brain, like the giant serpent supposed to haunt the water ways of Venus. But he was into his third bottle, and did not attend to it.

He ate, without appetite, a bowl of soup at a restaurant he knew, then walked on, up the streets. It was a boisterous night. The houses were all lighted up, huge flakes of brilliance falling from the latticed windows, out of the opened doors. Lanterns burned. Rose-sellers came to him, insinuating he went to a tryst, and trying to trade with him their flowers, which in the dark and light looked black, and smelled stagnantly perfumed as the canals. He bought one or two. He always did. From the most wretched.

Finally, there was the square before the Primo. An amazing religious procession was going over to the great church by firefly candlelight, little boys in white, and the galleons of the orthodox priests of the Virgin, in their magenta, the jeweled crosses raised up on a sea of flames, an icon of Beautiful Maria held before, veiled in the same blue sheen that flashed from the wings of a magpie

Furian watched. He felt lonely as a child. What had the song said: *Before her darkness ruled me.*

But all men were children alone, and in the dark.

The priests glided into the Primo, the crowd halted to make way like a vast glittering flood, dammed up by God, crossing their hearts, bowing.

A wanderer had come stealthily to the fence of gilded poles below the steps.

"Signore—do you want the boat again tonight?"

Furian turned. It was not the other—Juseppi?—but the man masked as a lion—with one visible squashed ear. Furian recognized the ear. The boatman was also excellent to have on hand in trouble, and would be worth sounding for Shaachen's Revel.

"Yes. The long ride we took before," said Furian.

"Up and down the canals? That's fine for me, Signore. The same rate?"

"Yes."

Furian got into the boat. He was no sooner in than across the enormous night looking-glass of the lagoon, into which all the topaz window-stars had trickled, the Song came drifting like a breeze. There was someone on another wanderer, a mandolin, a strong, clear tenor.

It cut to Furian through the layers of clothes and flesh and wine. It clutched his heart. Christ, the Song was so beautiful. It was a wonder, a gem. And the composer had died.

"That's a good tune," he said idly, to his ruffian boatman.

"Yes, Signore. It's surely caught on. They say it's played in the Archbishop's palace. Del Nero wrote it, but they think he's dead."

Furian thought, *The man who wrote this music—I reckoned him a boor, an effete poseur, a fool, likely to be killed and better for it. But he was touched by God.*

THE BLACK ROSES LAY on the floor of the boat.

Twelve had long since struck. They had found nothing. However, he had put to Squashed Ear the notion of attending Shaachen as a bodyguard, and the boatman had gladly agreed.

There was no moon. Stars slit the canals like knives.

Was it one, now? Morning? The lights were growing dim here, away from the great lagoons. So many black windows, or windows with just a faint bloom. So many lives, burning up or down, put out.

"Go that way."

"That canal? It's a bad place, there."

"You know it?"

"My cousin, he told me."

"Of course. But, just this once."

"You may be thankful I'm with you, Signore."

They went under the leaning houses, balconies. Here and there, an almost solitary lamp. The smell of the water was intense and horrible, a putrid tang under the accustomed foulness. He recalled the smell, which at the time he had not noticed. And there, the pinkish lantern on its hook.

He must have directed Squashed Ear indirectly, all this way, round and round, and in to this center. Unless he had mistaken. Certain parts of the City looked alike, even to one born here. Furian said, "Are we near to Fulvia?"

"No, no, Signore."

He was wrong then. Yet surely not. For there, exactly as it had been, over the wider pool of the canal, just before the narrowing of the way, that lighted window—The lattice of intricate small designs, like lace in the water.

A large house, one of the minor palaces, with high iron gates, and above the wall, the heads of old acacia trees, lending now an acid, resinous, autumnal odor.

They drifted by, and as they did, another boat, larger, came from some unnoted slip between the buildings, precisely into their wake.

Furian looked back. The second boat was mooring at the steps below the house, directly where the window reflected, The light fell clear on it, illuminating a fringed dark awning, brass fitments. There were six rowers. Furian heard the vague silky jangle of keys or bangles or chains.

"Get on, into the narrower canal," Furian said quickly. "Once we're out of the light, put down your oar."

Squashed Ear took this order without demur. Clearly he thought they were now after all on business. Perhaps they were. Just there, beyond the window, here now where the oar was going down to stay them in the mud, Juseppi had hooked the drowning mask out of the shadows.

Darkness enclosed the wanderer.

The water slop-slopped against the hull.

The gates of the house with the window were also catching light, opening. A servant came out with a lamp on a pole, like a melon-green moon hung halfway to the sky. And in its glow, his livery gleamed.

Then a woman's figure stepped between the gates and poised an instant above the water steps.

From his shadow, Furian watched. She was only thirty five or forty feet away, lit as if on a stage by the prow-lamp of the waiting boat, the moon-lamp by the garden gate.

Like the magpie Madonna, her gown was of that same, alien blue. Her skin, the tops of her breasts, were like white alabaster with yet one more lamp inside. Her hair looked the color of polished pewter, perhaps a wig, or metal powder. Her mask was a butterfly that covered all the face, its pin of body stretched from chin to hair-line, the wide outspread wings scattered with blue-eye markings, one pair of which would form the eyeholes for her own. There was something. What was it?

The wine buzzed angrily as bees in Furian's head. Impossible, stupid...

She was like the Song...

Piercing, the needle, sweet to pain. The colors, the textures, the way the lamp caressed her. Her graceful descent now into her boat.

And the oars started forward.

"They're coming up here, Signore."

"All right. Turn your mask away. We're waiting for someone else."

As the larger boat was rowed nearer, Furian partly turned his own head. He put his hand over the long, pointing nose of his mask, to conceal it.

The six-oared boat slipped by with the remotest tremor of the thick, mercurine water.

The most unnerving thing occurred. As the seated woman passed, some fluke of their light lit up a brilliant blue spark, as it seemed to be, from her eye inside the eye hole of the butterfly. It must have been a spangle.

But for three seconds, she was near enough to touch. He had the impulse to pick up the roses from the wanderer's floor and cast them over into her lap.

There were albino sapphires, two or three, fashioned like stars, netted in the metallic hair.

Her left hand, resting on the rail, was white and young. It had no rings.

The boat was past them and had gone around a bend of the canal. Its spine-ridged wake faded. Only the gentle slop-slop now again, on the hull.

"A bad woman," said Squashed Ear. He crossed himself.

"Your cousin knows her."

"He's heard tell."

She was a whore then. Did that explain everything? Del Nero had gone to a whore, fallen out with her or her manager, been robbed and stabbed and flung down in the canal?

Furian stared at the water, where the wake of the other boat had gone, and where the mask of the dark and white Apollo had floated, face up. Things were simple. They were always simple. He felt a sense of desolation, agonizing loss, so that a cry plunged in his chest, wanting to thrash up into the air. He coughed dryly instead.

"Yes, it stinks here, Signore."

\* \* \*

AFTER ALL, FURIAN SLEPT a couple of hours. Sometimes, on the fourth, fifth or sixth night without sleep, this happened.

At first, asleep, he was aware of the too-warm, gritty sheets, the uneven hardness of the mattress. Then that went.

He was in his father's house. He was fifteen, it was the day he composed the little harpsichord sonatella. His mother had played it, and they had applauded.

"This must be shown at the Temple. It should have a wider hearing." His father, proud and certain.

Now his mother and sister, in their white dresses. Was it spring in the dream? There was the scent of the statue-ed pool, and violets from the inner garden, and black dolche on a plate.

He said to his sister, older than he, "Why are your eyes so blue, Caro?"

"But my eyes aren't blue at all."

"Yes, bluer than violets."

He was very happy. He had never been curbed or treated unfairly. They had praised his achievements and bolstered his proper self-esteem. They had given him the True Religion, God, the Christ, the Virgin, and all the angels to care for him. He had beautiful clothes, lace on his shirts. He did not need to follow his father into the mercantile business which had made them rich. He could do what he chose, write music, write essays, walk among the charming wealthy people, attend to the fascinating adventurers who came into the house. One day he might select a lovely wife, or an adventure. He would want for nothing.

"My handsome boy," said his mother, all across the room. As a child, he had thought she, and his sister, the most gorgeous of all women. But now he knew there were other women more gorgeous, (as he knew there were other lands, and strange, discovered continents.) This did not make him love his kindred women less. He felt a tender pity for these first two sweethearts, now set a little aside for others more rare.

His mother sang—a bird trilled in its cage. The bird was blue as his sister's eyes, but the bird had been grey, and his sister's eyes dark.

There was no reason why such happiness and comfort, such security, such pleasure, should ever end. Their house was strong enough to withstand storms. His elder brother, for example, who had taken up with a girl of the streets. She had been removed to a good apartment, taught manners and fashion. She was now a flawless mistress, who blessed them all, prayed for them daily at a respectable mass. His own youthful indiscretions, (older than fifteen now), had been laughed over, smoothed over. His father: "My children are God's gift to me. I value them. They can do nothing I will turn my back on." They had eaten guinea fowl at breakfast, and white honey from the hives of their estate. Tonight they would dine on charcoaled boar, apples baked with cinnamon. There was to be a concert, a famous singer had arrived to entertain them. A ship had come in from far, far away, another world. There were bales of silk, better than even the East could produce, silk so fine it could be run, yards of it, through a woman's ring. And outside were the games of the City. And beyond the City the playground of the earth. There was nothing to fear. Even death would be kind, and a hundred masses said to make safe the soul. None of it need ever, ever end.

# 3

HE SPENT THE AFTERNOON and evening in Cupid's room. She was a prostitute, young and pretty, though not really to his secret taste, very slender, almost boyish, with short curly hair. She was skillful, but did not pretend, lying under him or over, if he preferred, with a calm friendly face. Once only, in an excess of desperation and lust, dead drunk and slow, he had made love to her for an hour before burying himself inside her. He had thought she was giggling, the curious bubbling sounds, until he understood she too had reached a crisis. She told him afterwards, abashed, she did not like this to happen. What she did was a sin, but the Virgin would forgive her, if she did not enjoy it. However, she offered at the shrines of Venus and Neptune, too.

Tonight, at the Revel of Diana, Furian knew what he was likely to see. He had needed to take off the aching edge.

Afterwards they sat eating apricots. He fed the fruit into her cunning little mouth.

"I wish you were rich, Furian. Then you could own me. Would you like to?"

"Nothing more," he said gallantly.

He knew—it was less affection than her desire to 'sin' only with one man.

Her bed in the dying light was the color of a dying pale yellow rose. She looked so young, but she was nineteen; she had told him her age two years ago.

She still wore her mask, which showed only the eyes, two swan wings threaded with cheap tinsel. He had hinged open his own mask, up to the nose, so he could kiss her. and eat an apricot.

"That makes you look like a duck, Furian!"

He thought of Juseppi, who had been a bull and a fish.

Between nine and ten, he dressed, and left her with a silver ducca. Downstairs, he went to the coffee shop near the Lamb Bridge, and waited for Squashed Ear to arrive.

A mandolin player was playing, badly, the melody of the Song Cloudio del Nero had composed. They would be sick of it in a week.

Squashed Ear was late. When he came, he looked not uncouth, black coat and black hat with a long blue feather. Furian had also dressed well, white stockings, the dark grey coat, and the hat with the grey plume. (He had, too, come armed.) Shaachen, he was aware, would dress in his worst best, the shirt with silver lace, earrings, God knew what else.

"Signore—I only discovered you by your long-nose mask'"

"Yes. You're late."

"Your pardon, Signore. There was a to-do by the Primo water steps. A priest had to come out."

"Oh, yes."

"It was a woman, a boatman's wife. She had fine tits but she was howling and tearing her hair.

"There's a drink."

"Thank you, Signore. I need it, I tell you. We

thought it was the usual—some man of us got her in the family way." Bored, Furian tossed back his brandy. "But it wasn't that. Shall I tell you, Signore?"

"If you like."

"Lost her husband, Signore. Gone missing. And she treated him like pig shit, was it any wonder. And Chomo, he says just this to her—the man's cousin, you understand, and she screams and screeches, pushed up his mask and rips his face with her claws. So Bollo runs to the Little Church by the Primo, and gets a priest, and the priest, he comes up, and he says, Quietly, daughter, you are a woman. But she only says, What do you know? *This* to a holy priest."

Furian had forgotten Squashed Ear was a gossip. In the long watches on the canals he tended to quietness, but became excited before other work. In his belt, was the sharp knife. He carried too a stout stave, as Furian had recommended.

"We'd better be going. He wants us at the Centurian's by eleven."

"Yes Signore. But isn't that like a woman. Doesn't want you when she has you. Goes crazy when you leave her. Of course, she's the boy at the University. He worked for the scholarship, but it took every penny Juseppi could put by—"

Furian paused. He glanced at Squashed Ear's lion mask.

"Juseppi, Signore, he's a steady one. I'd never have thought he'd go off and leave that sow, for all her bitchery."

"Maybe he found a nicer lady."

"Good luck to him then, Signore. Yes, good luck." And taking up Furian's bottle, Squashed Ear swigged from it heartily.

* * *

SHAACHEN WAS ALREADY AT the Centurion's Bridge. He was not, as he had said, on the Neptune side, where the small bearded idol stood in his niche, but on the Maria side, by the lighted image of the Virgin.

He wore a plain mask, and carried his heavy bag of tricks, which he immediately handed to Furian.

"Stick close."

"You're expecting trouble tonight."

"Always I expect it."

Squashed Ear slouched behind them.

There were black gulls flying, some twenty or thirty of them, across the panes of black sky between the houses, so also reflecting in the black panes of the canals. The moon had risen beyond Fulvia, over the sea.

"You see," said Shaachen to Furian, "I have an enemy here tonight." Furian said nothing. Shaachen said, "Take note. It's the Prince Teobalto."

"A prince, no less."

"A tall thin one, with a wig like a sheep's fleece, and the sheep inside it. He may have set minions to upset my work."

Soon they reached the arches that ran along beside the Equus Gardens, and Shaachen led them into the bar, where they drank wine.

They heard the Primo strike eleven.

Shaachen got up and they went on into the Gardens.

The public walks were busy with sellers of brandy and lemonade and riotous masked patrons. Between the cypresses and yews, the lamps shone like burning flowers. Three old gypsy women crept through the throng, with faces like clever parrots, selling charms. Shaachen brushed them off, but Squashed Ear fell behind a moment to purchase something. "Does he want it to assist kick or prick?" Shaachen muttered.

Steps led up to the high terraces of the Gardens. Here the only horses in Venus were kept luxuriously stabled in a lofty palace with a gilded chariot and four-horse team on its roof. They passed presently the ornate building, and next the wide enclosure where the blue rhinoceros stood, arrogant and forlorn beneath a juniper tree, staring back at those who stared at it. Over its tall railing ran a silver plaque, that proclaimed it a type of unicorn. Shaachen knew better and said so. The house of the white lions was noisy, although they had gone to bed. Their roars echoed fitfully over the Gardens.

There was a rhinoceros-lion smell too, mingling with the roses and night-blooming jasmine.

From here, you could look down and see the moon, round and edibly white. She posed now on the dome of the Primo, so they were momentarily twins.

Among the cedars, two police stood in their tricorn hats and dark garb. They flanked the marble archway that led through into the wild land beyond the Gardens, the Groves of Diana.

Shaachen, with his paper, got them by. But others would sneak through, over the low fences, among the thick, black-green trees. The Groves were a place of trysts.

Perhaps Juseppi was here with his mistress, the willing girl Furian had advised him to seek.

A white arm glimpsed among the night shrubs, but it was a statue. Few could make love to a stone.

Half a mile down, in the cultivated rough country beyond the gate, they easily discovered the Revel, which had already begun. It was an open pomegranate heart of

lamps and so-far civilized noises, with an orchestra playing. (On her plinth, marble Diana stood naked in her
drapery, two marble hounds at her heels, the sickle disc
on her forehead. Her cold eyes looked indifferently
away.)

It was the prince Teobalto, also plain-masked, and
seemingly with, as Shaachen had prophesied, a piled
sheep upon his head, who came mincing to greet them,
with two satyr youths in silks and myrtle crowns gambol-
ing after.

"You are here, dear Doctor. Do you have miracles
with you?"

"Of course, Signorissimo. Everything's to hand."

"I expect great marvels. Better than your show for
Floriano."

"Ten times better, Signorissimo. Or strike me."
Shaachen winked offensively.

Wine came, nosegays.

Furian looked long, and slowly, all about him. His
eyes made for him a shifting tapestry of lambent dresses,
coats, hair piled in false clouds, the flicker and stab of
jewels. And to this, the orchestra played accompaniment
so mathematically, like a mechanical toy. It had four
dolls, at tabor, at fiddle, at trumpet, even a harpsichord
balanced on a floor of planks. While everywhere, half-
disembodied and alive on their own, the masks of
Carnival. A true unicorn to make any rhinoceros blush.
A maned tiger. Gargoyles, Neptunes, dryads. And the
fashionable new masks that were like fans, their spread
tines rising into the plumes of peacocks and flamingos.

Furian had known all this, something close to it,
only those few years since. He missed it still, the comforts
and allurements, the sweet fragrances of pampered
washed skin, and perfume from the Orient. He rubbed

his sores against the splinters of his loss, viciously cherishing everything he might no longer have.

"Look there," said Shaachen. "Look, look."

"What? Which?"

"Her mask—the Principessa Messalina."

"You know their names, not I."

"The blond gown clasped with opal."

Furian looked. She was a tall woman, whose ziggurat of hair matched her dress. The mask was a wonder. A fan, but of fretted ivory, out of which partly emerged the outlines of a delicious ivory face, with dawn lips and evening lids.

"She has, herself, the countenance of an ox," said Shaachen. "No doubt the mask suits her better. Made, they say, such masks, by an inner circle of the Mask Guild. I've heard she keeps it on in bed, her husband, the prince, prefers it. Her lover, too."

Shaachen also was an old gossip. Furian turned away, to where a monkey was jumping over a cane, higher and higher, with apparent good will.

Beyond the monkey, at the edge of the clustering trees, blue glimmered on darkness.

He said, lightly, to Shaachen, "And who is that one?"

"Oh, caught your fancy, has she? I thought you only liked the bad girls, Furian Furiano."

"So I do. Isn't she bad at all?"

"Not with your sort. But I don't know her. Yes, a graceful line. But too slight. What does she live on, honeydew?"

Squashed Ear leaned forward. "There's supper over there. The sort of food I don't often see."

"Eat," said Shaachen, "don't gorge. There may be work to do."

Squashed Ear strode boldly behind the rows of

dainty gilded chairs, to long tables holding pagodas of fruit, and a terrible greenish salt-swan from the lagoons, stuffed with spicy fish, no doubt, and dressed in its feathers. There came a rearrangement about the orchestra.

A goblet of Venusian crystal was in Furian's hand. Impossible turquoise glass blown with vapors like cirrus. He stared at it. He did not want this moment, because he knew now they would sing the Song. And she—she stood there against the trees in her alien blue. The woman whose eyes held blue fire.

He drank quickly. The wine was ancient and heady. It lifted up his skull so the moon, which now was sailing closer over the groves, could see in at his brain.

A little boy dressed as a Roman page was standing before the harpsichord stage. He had the fine, pinched face and pouter pigeon chest of a diver's child. They were trained to develop their lungs for swimming long segments of time under Aquila and Silvia, searching out drowned treasures of Venus. Sometimes one would be found instead to have a voice,

The orchestra rippled, and the mincing Prince Teobalto called out shrilly, like an elderly lady at the play, "Hush! Hush, if you please!"

Twittering, the party went silent, and the Song began.

He should watch her. Watch her butterfly mask, watch for the flame of blue tears escaping the eyeholes. Or would tell-tale blood, also as in a play, appear on her fingers or her gown?

With the orchestra supporting it, like a transparent bird, the child's voice—he had one, indeed—flew up the delicate notes.

Furian now heard all the words.

In his darkness, having found her, he could only try

to win her. But she would not smile, he could not make her smile. Not at a jest, not in happiness, not even out of compassion. And so he must leave her to her solitary stony fate, and himself could only die.

At the last word, the boy held the note, long and long, the orchestra whispering, garlanding the silk-drawn hurt of its beauty. The audience held its breath. The vulgar ones counted. Not needing to count, Furian knew the child held the note for one whole minute, until he mildly signaled with hand, the orchestra coiled up the Song, and his voice sank effortlessly to an end.

They fell on him like loving hyenas, petting, stroking. The child, not out of breath, suffered it with dignity, until his gaudy guardian came up to lead him away.

The tears had pierced from Furian's own eyes. They had burnt him where they got out. The long-nosed mask hid everything.

But she stood immobile by the trees. Her own mask would hide nothing, for why should she care. And he himself was not moved, forgivably, by human tragedy, only by the power of music.

Shaachen said urgently, "Wake up. Fetch that lout." And primly, "How dare he use the nobles' tables as a trough? He should have gone to the servants' station. I must go down now and prepare."

IN THE BEGINNING, Furian had been intrigued by Shaachen's alchemical and sorcerous talents, but he was too skilled. If they were tricks, you could not see through them, and if the magic were real, they inspired an idea of horror. What kind of world was it where evil and humiliation prevailed, yet a sun could be made to rise from a bowl of water?

# The Mask

The country was very wild here, had been let go, the trees enormous, primal flowers in long, tasseled grass, and here and there a statue artfully toppled, its hands snapped off, girdled by moss.

In a clearing, lit now by the moon, Shaachen went to a marble altar. It was perhaps fifty years old, looked a thousand, cracked and weathered, with ivy. Trees closed thick behind it.

Shaachen snatched his bag, and threw out handfuls of powder. He made over the altar three or four passes. Squashed Ear watched respectfully, suppressing belches.

"He's a gifted and wise man." Furian shrugged. Squashed Ear added, "I wouldn't like to get on his shadow side."

"Nor would he like you to. Just keep an eye open for anyone trying to spoil things."

The Revelers were eddying down after them now. The Princess Messalina came first, with a man on either arm. She was laughing raucously, tossing her head. The ivory mask had made her playful. Which was the husband and which the lover? Neither of either? Others followed, and some men with torches,

The orchestra did not come, only the tabor man with his narrow drum. He stood to one side, and began to tap a rapid little heartbeat.

The sparkling crowd surged and swirled. It was smaller. Not all had followed.

Prince Teobalto appeared, his silk covered by a long black robe, and his face, now, by a ram's mask with gilded curling horns to augment his fleece. He was to be High Priest of the Revel.

Furian felt a weary distaste. Once or twice, with Shaachen, he had watched such affairs before. At one, even, a lamb had been put to death, a 'sacrifice' which

47

was unlawful, (Not for any ethical reason, the Butcher's Guild opposed it.)

The torches were planted in the ground in ready slots.

Youths dressed as pagan altar boys lined up behind Teobalto. He raised his arms. The black sleeves swooped back and showed anachronistic lace.

"O Diana, look kindly on your worshippers."

No one mocked his old-lady voice.

Shaachen, tucked in by a tree, touched something in his bag.

A shower of silvery lights sprayed upwards from the altar, formed the shape of a crescent moon, and went out.

The crowd chirruped and lifted its cups of Venusian glass.

A part-naked girl came out of the wood at the altar's back. She was white and slender, with large, firm breasts. At her groin hung a fringe of scintillants, and she was wigged and masked in silver.

She leapt lightly on the altar, gestured to the sky. She sang a verse.

"Kneel and honor her, the goddess of the night."

Furian thought, *Where is the blue whore? I don't see her.*

More silver rain dazzled up. The naked girl now danced slowly, describing her body with her hands, and the Revelers swayed as if before a snake. Furian felt no desire. In the crowd he could not see the girl in alien blue. She must be above, her butterfly hinged up, eating and drinking with a greasy mouth. There were several who had no interest in *this*, preferred more private dalliance. Perhaps she was choosing for herself another victim. As they said, *The canals are deep.*

The first girl lay flat on the altar, and a shining crescent rose out of her body and burst in streaks of pale fire.

A hunting horn sounded deep in the wild park.

Now, then, for the show-piece.

Furian glanced about. Shaachen's way seemed clear. Why in any case would Prince Teobalto work out a grudge on Shaachen, who was less than a gnat to him, and here of all places?

Then the goddess Diana came racing from the wood.

She must be an illusion, but how conjured God knew. Yes, Shaachen had genius as well as villainy. Maybe he was even in league with some supernatural power, as the alleys said.

Diana was tall, perhaps seven or eight feet in height. Her hair poured back from a diamond fillet, and the lunar crescent was iridescently blazoned on her forehead. She wore a tunic and buskins, as in certain paintings. She was white as snow, as the moon, all but her diamonds, and her eyes which burned a feverish nocturnal yellow-green, like a cat's. Behind her ran, or seemed to run, the white lions of the Equus

The crowd scattered with exclamations.

Diana bounded over the altar and the cowering mortal girl, blew right through the clearing, and her train of lions and dogs after her, and other animals out of myth, even an icy unicorn, whose glacial horn gleamed like a drawn sword.

They were gone in a lightning through the Groves.

The guests of Prince Teobalto righted themselves in clamor, laughing and blaspheming. The prince himself, the High Priest, straightened from a terrorized crouch.

The tabor player, who had lost the beat, regained it.

Was this all? No. Another apparition was walking out of the wood.

A voice, better by far than Teobalto's, (trained), announced, "The folly of life. The unreason of flesh. These have brought you here. Behold."

The apparition halted. It was a woman in a dress of black velvet traced by jewels. Was she actual? Perhaps not. An unearthly music quivered, pipes, harps, to the rhythm of the tabor—which perhaps was no longer being played.

She wore, this creature, a fan mask, and all at once, drew it off. Beneath, another mask, this like a woman's face, rouged and powdered, with spangled lids. She drew off the second mask. Now her face was stretched, pure skin, taut as that of a young girl, yet sallow, like parchment. The eyes smoldered black. And then she pulled off the mask of skin. Below was the skull.

It was an ornate skull, set with a green jewel between the eyes. But the eyes were gone. Two hollows, like the black night hollow of the wood beyond the altar. White teeth grinned, lipless.

The androgynous voice announced, "Ah, what matter the world's sorrow. Smile, smile, Signorissimas, Signorissimos. I, a skull, tell you. Keep smiling. *I* do!"

The figure winked out. It had looked solid, but was a phantom. Again, Furian pondered how it was done—a mirror in the wood, some image cast by lamps from another place...

One of the ladies was fainting. But the Princess Messalina had pranced forward in her ivory mask.

She vaulted on to the altar, and with two hands ripped apart the bodice of her costly gown. Two fallen breasts slid from the cage of corseting.

Messalina laughed. She stamped her foot on the altar. There was something quite mad about her. Something—unholy.

A thick-set man, masked and maned as a wolf, ran forward and seized her, dragged her down, screaming and laughing, and galloped her away into the wood from which the apparitions had emerged.

Furian stepped back.

Couples cantered past him. A naked, eagle-faced man hustled the naked girl from the side of the altar—and a wonder the princess had not trodden on her—his hands already busy on her flesh.

The sight of a skull had seemed to make them appreciate the flesh a great deal—

Teobalto, the ram, leaned on a tree, with one of his acolytes kneeling before him, the priestly black robe bundled up over his head.

Squashed Ear spat. Furian said sharply, "Control yourself. Don't be a fool."

Shaachen, like an over-dressed, demented gutter rat, sprang up to them. "They've ruined my show. I had more. We go now. Shake this dust off our heels."

The gilded horns of the ram scraped bark audibly. Already shrieks of orgasm spumed from among the trees.

A woman with a nymph mask and green tresses, half unclothed, rushed against Furian.

"Feel me! *Touch* me!"

But he put her off, and went by.

As they climbed up the slope, Shaachen scurrying ahead, cursing, muttering like a granny cheated of her treat, the form of the woman in the blue dress appeared. She stood solitary, unique, like a ghost. Tonight there were pearls in her hair. She clasped her hands lightly together at her so-narrow waist. He could have snapped her in half. The butterfly of her face showed only the most distant hint of eyes. Were they blue, or black? Or nothing, like the skull.

Shaachen fussed past her, not seeming to see. Squashed Ear strode after. In a covet beyond, a small rosy boy, unclad like a cherub, had unleashed his own desire on a pie. He rent it like a savage beast a deer, the gravies splashing like blood.

Furian said, "Who are you, Madama?"

Her masked face stirred a little, a blue-white flower on a stem. She said nothing.

Furian said, bleakly, "Keep smiling, Madama."

And went on up the slope.


"THE GOD WAS TO COME, the deus of Carnival. Lust." Shaachen chattered as they climbed up the inner stair. The lower floor lay in lightless disarray after his latest clinic. "Then the planets of the City, Maxima Venus, Neptune for Pesci, and the moon for Cancro, and Vulcan for Scorpio. Ultimately, fireworks, without powder, naturally. But these drunken licentious sots, they can't wait. They must have off their garments and rut."

"Perhaps they were afraid of your powers."

"Afraid? He demanded it all, that booby."

"Teobalto. He didn't cause trouble."

"I expected to be set on. Certain things—showed I would be. And he, he's joined the Alchemist's Guild. He reckons to become a master, but even a rose petal in water, to make it move's beyond him. He's jealous."

Shaachen flung open his upper door.

The study loomed, dim as a tunnel, until Shaachen struck tinder to the candles. There was the clatter of wings.

"Ah, my darling. How are you? Did you miss me?" Shaachen, calmed at once by his familiar, stroked the magpie's demoniac head. "Tell me what time is it?"

The magpie, from its perch on his shoulder, split the black clippers of its beak and cawed twice.

"Ah," said Shaachen, "what minutes?"

The magpie shook its head, ruffled the black and white wings. Under its dagger beak and wicked head, its feathered breast was soft as a baby's first hair.

"None then," said Shaachen. He held up his hand. "Hark."

They paused, and after some thirteen seconds, heard the Primo strike the second hour of morning.

The magpie was infallible in its trick of telling time. It would even demonstrate the minutes, hopping or pecking up to thirty, raising the left wing to indicate the lapse before, the right to show the minutes after, the hour.

One more uncanny feat.

The colored bottles and vials massed black on the window. The bird had knocked one over.

Shaachen took the cover from a reeking dish of unpleasant scraps, and fed the magpie, which ripped and tore eagerly.

"He'll pay me. I'll make him pay."

"Meanwhile I must convey your thanks to the boatman below."

"Oh, give him what you want from this." Shaachen tossed a bag of silver into Furian's hand.

"You're generous again."

"I'm rich. You know it. Why have you never robbed me, Furian Furiano?"

"It would tire me, Doctor Shaachen. It's less wearing to be good."

Shaachen chortled, in a better humor feeding disgusting entrails to his bird. "Did you make a meeting with your blue skinny?"

He did not miss much.

"No. She didn't want me, as you warned."

"Courage. Perhaps she'll change her mind. I locked it up."

"What, Doctor, did you lock up?"

"That mask you brought. You see?" He pointed to a high cupboard, reachable only by steps, set like a jail among the squeeze of books.

Furian said, "You lost interest in it."

"No. My interest grows. It's a horrid, nasty thing, that mask. It carries a taint."

"A composer of a song wore it," said Furian.

"Songs!" said Shaachen. "It stinks of some awful-ness."

"How?" asked Furian, despite himself. He had not wanted to think about the mask from the canal, the mask of Cloudio del Nero. But there was no chance in any case. His music sprouted everywhere, like a divine weed.

"Imagine," said Shaachen, "a gazelle with the head of an adder. Imagine an angel, with the wings of a moth, broken, falling. Imagine unseen scratching on a window."

"The mask."

"The mask knows an infamous secret. It holds the secret of the death. The filthy joke of some filthiest god."


GULLS WERE FIGHTING in the sky. The tide was lushly in, smelling of sea and offal, and water sipped at the brink of the pavement.

Furian gave Squashed Ear his fee. Squashed Ear lingered "Those women. Those noble ladies. I heard they go with any one." Roused up, evidently.

Furian said, "Better get home and wake your wife."

"I'd rather wake Juseppi's wife."

Furian said, "The best fortune, then," and was turning to go, when he saw darkness-on-legs coming round from the wall of Shaachen's palace.

Below, the high canal, the pole with the Neptune and no boat tethered. One lamp, smashed, giving no light, and the moon down. It was Shaachen's lofty window which lit the scene.

"A difficulty," said Furian, to Squashed Ear. "We'll have to earn our money after all."

There were four of them, big fellows from the rubbish tips of the lagoons. He had a view of stained, welcoming teeth, an earring that glittered, and knives that glittered better. Then Shaachen's candles went out one by one above, the window died, and there was no light at all.

*Thank you, Doctor.*

As they lurched nearer, Furian saw that three came dedicatedly for him, as if to a prescribed meeting.

His belly was molten, but his hands were always steady at such a juncture. It was after he would shake. If he lived to do it.

He said, "Gentlemen, come on. Can't I buy you off?"

One stood grinning like the keep-smiling skull, in front of him. Two nudged closer either side, more serious.

Furian took a handful of the ink-stanching writer's sand he brought out with him on such nights from his coat pocket. He slung it in the solemn left-hand face, at the eyeholes of the half mask. Simultaneously pulled the knife free of his belt, and rammed it in the middle one's guts.

To the left, hawking, scrabbling at eyes. The other, still grinning under a paste-board nose, bowed over, his teeth darkening further in the darkness, from blood.

The third one was surprised. His own blade tore Furian's best coat as Furian stamped—the gesture of the sex-avid principessa—on his foot. Then Furian had got the hand with the knife. He dislocated three fingers, and as the man romped glugging sideways, cut the fatal vein in his neck.

He kicked sand-eyes in the chest, smashing the breast bone. It gave as easily as the rib of a cooked fowl.

The other one, the fourth, was standing over Squashed Ear, who lay full-length. His head had been stoved in, and the proud hat, the feather, were wet and bruised like a fruit from the mess inside.

"Fuck you," said Furian. He leaned forward and sliced the fourth man's mask and face wide open. But through his blood, dropping down, the fourth man flatly said, "*We'll see*—"

And out of the shadow again, like fresh pus from a bottomless wound, more of them were coming, five, six, seven, hissing and rumbling, and some light that did not exist snagging the quills of their knives.

Furian turned. He jumped off the pavement, straight down into the stinking hell-black cold of the canal.

Below, the water insistently closing, holding tight to mouth and nostrils and breath to shut it out.

He surfaced ten lengths along the waterway, and two knives plopped in beside him like friendly fish.

Then some stone they had plucked, unreasonably momentous, struck him a numb and deathly blow to the right side of his back.

Furian sank now, gasping in the poison of the canal, swallowing the piss of the sea god's night.

*Christ and Maria*—A bodily surge tried to eject the

muck at once. His nose and throat were full of liquid ordure going two ways.

Choking, he came up, gagged, spat, went under a third time.

He swam in a panic-bright trance of oblivious, nauseous confusion. He kept down as long as he could.

Emerging finally he knocked against the stone of a house-side, and a little rat went neatly by him, happy in its element.

But the bullies someone had sent to crown the night were almost far enough away. Around a turn or two of the canal.

Furian forced himself down once more and swam until consciousness was almost out.

He came up by some ancient stair he did not recognize. No lamps, the rope-arteries of alleys. Fruit peel rotted on the water.

Under the wall, he thrust off his mask, sneezed violently twice, then brought up the fluid of half the canal, garnished by Cupid's apricots. Far above someone cursed him for a drunk. He crawled away down an alley, back full of black pain, retching and laughing, part strangled, wiping the slime from his eyes.

# 4

A FAT PRETTY DAUGHTER of the Amari family, who he had fancied once, and once been allowed to fondle—but no more than fondle, she was virtuous—observed him without comment. She had a pretty mask too, a pink flower with eyes.

Then she said, as he turned for the door, "You shouldn't bath in your clothes, Signore."

"You'll have to show me how to do it properly one day, Fiamina."

She said, "Two men came, just after dawn."

"Two men—for me?"

"Yes, Signore. They wanted your rooms. They had something for you, they said."

"Did you show them?"

"Mumma did. All up the stairs."

"Are they up there now, Fiamina?"

"No. They came out. They were sorry to miss you."

Nothing was out of place in either of the two rooms. On the table was a duplicate of his mask, a white face with a long, pointing nose. It had been skewered to the wood by a cheap stiletto.

That was all.

It was enough. He was the mask. They had noted him, and would complete the task.

As he was rowed towards the Primo, Furian could smell the carpentry smell of Signore Amari's second coat. He had bought it from him soon after returning to the apartment. Amari had wanted Furian's best clothes too, even though Furian had been roaming in them, wet and stinking, for nearly three hours. He had taken a long and rambling way home. Not that it was home any longer.

The locked box that contained his books, the green glass and his mother's mirror—all he cared about—he left with the caretaker under some coins. "Not for sale." He left his rent too, sufficient for another month. By then something would have happened. He would be dead, or elsewhere, or all the trouble settled, whatever the bloody trouble was. For while Shaachen's (perhaps imagined) feud with Prince Teobalto might account for a roughing up, the band by the canal had been merchants of death.

He was cruelly sorry about Squashed Ear. He did not even know his true name, but presumably there was a widow.

It was another man's wife, however, that he meant to see.

When he stepped ashore below the heavenly white dome, no one took much notice. His clothes had the laborer's look, and his mask was different, a black dog's short pugnacious snout, complete with whiskers.

They had known the other mask. They had been at pains to show him so.

Of course, they could have waited. Bribed the

Amaris to keep quiet. (Would the Amaris have done that? Probably.) Whoever wanted Furian so much was also in no hurry, perhaps even enjoyed this game with a quarry who changed his appearance and ran stealthily away.

"Is Juseppi about?"

"No. No one's seen Juseppi for a week."

"A day," said another.

A third wanderlier, a big man, came up whistling the Song. It was an omen. He bulked before Furian and said, "Hey, Doggy, I can tell you something. What's it worth?"

"What's the news?" said Furian, "and I'll let you know."

The big man, masked as Juseppi had been, but better, as a large bloated fish, hinged up his mask to reveal a fishy, thick-lipped mouth. "Clever, for a dog."

Furian said, "I heard he was in difficulties."

"So what? You're a carpenter from Silvia, I'll bet. What's a wanderlier to you?"

Someone, negating the omen, pushed the big fish aside and said straight out to Furian, "I heard he died, Juseppi. I was going by this morning. There was a row from his house. He had half the ground floor of the Palace Bertro. From his wife's family, you see. But she was screaming away. She's got a loud voice. It was Oh God, my Juseppi, what shall I do?"

"She's a slut," said another, "came down here, making a dance. She's got an eye for a man."

"Watch out, if you go there," said another.

"The Palace Bertro?"

"See, he wants to go there now, meet her. It's on the Blessed Maria Canal. Just behind the Little Church."

Dressed as he was, he should have very poor supplies of money, so he gave them nothing, and walked off, to barks and cries of encouragement.

The Blessed Maria Canal ran narrow and glass-green, and on the balconies above were flowers with the washing. The Palace Bertro had a courtyard before it, where an old woman sat in black like a suitable specter. She had a black cloth mask.

She paid him no heed. Everything was quiet. He went in at the door and was in a large room, its plaster peeling, shimmering with the water reflection through tall latticed windows. Three lean cats eyed him from a passage way out of which now rose a dull, ominous murmur. Then a woman wailed, long and rasping. It sounded more like fury than distress. He had come to the right place.

He knocked at an old door. There was silence now.

After a minute, a thin boy opened the door. He had lank fair hair and a terrified unmasked face. He wore the charcoal gown of the University. He was about fourteen.

"Juseppi," said Furian, clearly.

"My father."

"Will you let in."

"No, Signore. No, no."

"I want to help your mother."

"No—no—"

Then, behind the boy, a woman came sweeping and pushed the door wide. Her black hair was half up, half down. She wore a black lace veil over it, askew, and wrapped across her breasts that two men had praised. Her eyes were rusty from tears, her unmasked face coarse, beautiful, lined and raging.

"Who are you? What? Tell me! What do you know?"

"Nothing, Signora. I used his boat now and then."

"Then why are you here?"

"I was concerned."

She flung back her head on the rounded column of her fawn throat. She laughed roughly. The disheveled veil slipped and she yanked it back.

He saw her eyes were also half insane. There was a sort of blindness in their depths—she had been shown some thing that had made it hard for her to look at anything else, or give anything else her judgment.

"Oh come in. Come in. What do I care?"

The boy moved away from the door, and Furian walked into the room.

It was wide and gracious, like the chamber outside, with a terra-cotta floor, and one vast window where a glorious pot of basil  towered. At a long table two men with eye-masks sat sullenly, grim-faced, and in the corner was another old woman, masked and wearing black, exactly like the one outside.

Things were scattered. A mending box, very full, (he could not picture her mending), a broom, a chest, open, and spilling sleeves, an overturned stool, soiled dishes set on the floor.

"Have some wine," said Juseppi's wife, loudly, scornfully. "Why not?"

"Calypso," chided one of the men. He got up but at once she let out again a huge almost inhuman scream.

"Leave me alone! In God's name, haven't I earned it."

And she tore her hair, violent, so a slender strand of it came loose in her grip. She waved this at Furian. "I'm not to be trifled with. Not now."

Furian said, "What happened to him?"

"Oh? You want to know that? You do?"

"Yes, Signora."

"Come here then. Yes, come and look."

And she reached out and grasped his hand in her

his pipe, "it was the Snake. It chomped him in bits with
its teeth."

Hands rose, crossing hearts. They were superstitious, the wanderliers, about the giant supernatural serpent under the lagoons and canals of Venus.

Furian said, "Had he done something to anger it?"

"Anger *someone*," said the unmasked dolphin. "He'd
found something, blabbed about it."

"Found what?"

"He'd rowed a man about, looking for Carnival
corpses for some cranky alchemist."

"What man?"

"God knows. But Juseppi found a mask."

"No ordinary mask," said the other man, who had
his eyes part covered by owl wings. He put down his
fuming pipe, took the brandy bottle and filled his own
glass.

"A mask's a mask," said Furian.

"This one was a-drip with evil," said the man.

"How?"

"He didn't say. He said he dreamed of it all night.
It—howled at him. He said it was a portent of his death.
He went to confess at Primo Suvio."

Furian's ears roared softly. The lights of the tavern
swam through the air. The swallowed canal water had
not done him good.

"Well, that's enough for me. If he's gone, she'll be
lonely."

"Calypso? Not she. Heard tell she'd got another
admirer already."

Furian got up unsteadily. They laughed and gave
him a supportive shove. The dizziness passed and he
walked jauntily out of the tavern.

There was no one in the street. He thought of the

child scrubbing at plates. Probably, under her dress, she was black and blue with her mother's beatings.

You wanted to rescue them, all of them. But it was not possible. For everyone seen, there were a thousand more. All those blows, those tears. And God in his jewel-encrusted heaven, looking down, missing not even the fall of the sparrow. Smiling at its pain?

Juseppi had talked generously about the mask. He had made a confession of his sins. He had thought the mask foretold his death. It had.

Furian walked slowly. Long and warm and raw, the shadows of the houses slopped on him, and the noon sun sword-slanted between. It would be easy to drop down flat.

Like the slices of light and dark, the pieces of all this, whatever it was, swung round him. He glanced over them.

The mask lay on the water just beyond the reflection of a window. Cloudio del Nero's mask. The window of the blue harlot. And Juseppi on the bed, in ten or eleven parts. While the knives of would-be assassins glittered like the quills of porcupines, and again the stone struck him in the back, and he gulped the urine of Neptune and went down.

Furian leant on a wall. He needed some medicine. Shaachen would be excellent for that—Get to Shaachen.

But then, Shaachen was also caught inside the swirling of loose bright pieces. Del Nero's mask was in his cup board. Surely it was the mask which must give up the answer to all this?

# 5

CUPID SAID, "IF I PAY HIM, why won't he come? Look. I've got eighty-seven silver duccas saved, and all these brass venuses. Surely he would? You're not fit—"

"He wouldn't, Cupid. But you're a winged angel to say it. I shouldn't be here."

"Where else but with me, that likes you so?"

Furian lay on her bed, in the rose-death sheets, staring stupidly at the ceiling. His dog mask was on the floor but she still had the swan wings over her eyes, which were dark and anxious. A good actress.

He had gone to her by devious routes. Everybody went to prostitutes, for God's sake, it should be safe for her. Anyway, if questioned, she would betray him at once. It would be a code, not to be sentimental, and kind only where able.

She had been kind this afternoon. Putting off a client, albeit an elderly one she disliked, giving Furian clean water and the juice of plums. He no longer vomited, but the slight nausea dragged on. She said he had a fever, a white fever. She had sucked and licked at him until he jetted into her mouth, saying this would help to cleanse him. She was an adorable girl, with her gilded curly head, like a slender cherub. Of course, he paid her well. Some of the eighty seven duccas were his.

"Your Doctor Dianus is a beast," she finally concluded, "if he wouldn't visit you. And you're his friend."

"Maybe. Yes, perhaps. Or no."

He wanted to wait until the night came. He had a plain black eye-mask and a different coat, bought from a desperate Jewish tailor near Aquila. It was an elegant coat. Not his usual style at all.

There had been no one he had suspected, no attack all day. Probably he had built events into a ridiculous importance. They were all coincidences elevated by the fever.

When the sun set, he sat up, and waited for the room to steady.

"You don't sweat enough. It should pour out of you to rinse off the poison. Those canals. They kill so many. Even a crab from there can kill you, if you eat it not hot enough. And you, to go *swimming* there."

"I was pissed as a king, my Cupid."

"Silly Furian."

She kissed him, and then helped him to dress.

"Don't—be careful who you speak to, Cupid."

"Oh? What's up?"

"I owe a man money."

Outside the sky was magpie (alien) blue, and stars made patterns that fever-moved now, fascinating him.

He would go across Fulvia. He would, better yet, take the other route first.

Something said within him, rankled, like the sober voice in drink, *Don't be a fool.*

He laughed it off, as one did the sober voice. To hell with it. He would.

\* \* \*

THE CANAL TURNED, and they came into wider water. On either side the phosphorescent dimness of houses like cliffs. Iron balconies. Night-faded white roses from an urn.

The lamp burned. No longer pink. It was grey, now.

As Juseppi had, the wanderlier started to sing, not the Song.

*"If you were mine, my girl—"*

"Shut up," said Furian.

"Signore?"

"I don't want to offend you. But don't sing."

"Very well, Signore."

They were usually polite, in the boat. They wanted the fare. This one had the visage of a clown. It leered out of the shadow, its frown and down-turned mouth.

The window was above them. It was black.

"Put down the oar."

"Signore?"

A stupid one, this.

"Stop us here. Wait, until I tell you."

Furian stood up. The influx of new drink had contained the vertigo of the fever.

He looked at the window, and readied himself. It showed very little, only one faint-gleaming thing, just behind the lattice. Which might be anything.

Furian sang. His voice, untrained but sound, a light baritone.

*"She is the moon of my evening.*

*"Before her darkness ruled me."*

He knew the song. He sang it, both verses, with a slow intensity; largo. He wanted to make her smile, could not. She would not. He must die. He held the last note only for nine seconds, and when he stopped, there was a spike in his left side. But it went away.

"Oh Signore—bravo, bravissimo—"

"Quiet. Be quiet."

The gleaming faint thing was her mask, the butterfly with blue eyes and eyeholes for blue eyes.

In the moment he realized, he realized too she was not wearing it. It hung there in space, suspended by a ribbon from some hook, behind the lattice in the shadow.

He spat in the canal, and remembered he had only thought the truth—but what?—it was forgotten—under the unlucky Bridge of Lies.

SHAACHEN'S PALACE WAS IN DARKNESS, and when he went around to the alley door, it was locked. Furian knocked a while. Shaachen had occasional servants, you could never be sure. On the wall someone had scrawled *Death to Lovers!*

When no one came to open up, Furian forced a narrow, weak-grilled window to the side.

He climbed in, went through a verminous pantry, and up a back stair. Twice he had had to use this way before.

The door to Shaachen's study was ajar, and inside there was no sound.

"Doctor Shaachen—are you there?"

Shaachen's voice muttered, elderly, hollow. "Who would know?"

"Furian."

"Come in and see." Furian went through the door. Doctor Dianus Shaachen, seated in the corner on the floor, looked up and said, "Am I? Am I Shaachen?"

The room was lit by one guttering lamp. It was a shambles.

The window that faced the canal, black now, had stayed intact, but all the bottles were broken. On the ground lay the orrery, buckled and ruined. Books were everywhere, torn, pages trampled, and smeared with excrement which stank, in a dry, thin way, hours out of date.

On the desk the heavy tortoise-turtle had not been harmed, but papers were scattered, some drawn, Furian could see, with crude moronic cartoons of sex and savagery.

A chair had been smashed.

Furian's eyes went up the wall, past a broken lamp. and found the cupboard like a jail, where the books had been pulled down. The cupboard door was off, hanging by one hinge. The place inside was empty.

"They took the mask."

Shaachen said, "Curse the mask. Do I want it. What does it matter to me, the death of human debris.."

"He was—" said Furian. He stopped. In Shaachen's hands, as he sat on the floor like a tired child, was something black and white, stiff, and oddly folded like a poorly made cloth doll.

"You see," said Shaachen. He held it up. The lamp stroked a pearly gleam along white feathers, the shine of the canals over black ones. "They didn't touch him. He flew up too high, my darling. But when I came back, and come in, and find it, when I find all this, he flies down to me. Down to me, his father. And he puts his head into my breast. And then he dies. It was anger kills him, or fear. My darling. My only love. My magpie."

"Christ, Christ," said Furian.

"Fucks on your Christ. Where was your Christ when my darling died? Shits on him."

Furian went to the table. A decanter of deep blue

Venusian glass held wine. He poured it in a goblet and took it to Shaachen.

"You drink. Would choke my throat."

Shaachen lifted the dead magpie to his lips and kissed the smoke-soft feathers. Its black eyes glistened, not yet dull.

Furian swallowed wine. He took more. He sat down by Shaachen on the floor. It was very dark, the lamp purple with exhaustion, nothing in the window but broken bottles and black sky.

"Gather your strength, Doctor. We should leave here. They wanted the mask, and might come back to punish you."

"What do I care. Let them come. I'll rip out their livers."

"That might not be possible."

"Let me alone."

They sat side by side, and the magpie rested stiff and weightless with death in Shaachen's old hands. The lamp filmed, flickered and went out.

Just audible, as if made louder by the lessening of sight, the glutinous constant murmur of the canal reached in to them. The sea would, in the end, wash the City away, would wash away everything.

Shaachen began slowly and carefully to speak. He told how he had seen the magpie in a too-little cage in the market, and how he had fed it a scrap of meat. And then they had let the magpie sit on his wrist and the magpie had pecked Shaachen spitefully, and the vendor swore at it and pulled on its leg chain hurtfully to correct it. But Shaachen had said, "Give him me." For the magpie had spirit and had been ill-treated, and anyway, was Shaachen's lost child. He told how he loved the magpie, its beauty, its strengthening flights about his rooms. How

he took it to his bed, where it perched on the bedpost,
nestled on his pillow, shat on the Eastern carpet and his
wig on its stand. He loved its unmusical voice, its grace
and insolence, its musty sometimes rancid smell. It came
to know him. It trusted him. He alone could handle it,
and when it pecked him he scolded it, then took it in his
hand and kissed its bristly and wicked head. Its breast
was warm and soft as a girl's. You could feel the heart
beating like a tiny drum. It strutted and poked about.
Once it had relieved itself on his dinner and then, with a
delicate beak, eaten the compendium. You could feel its
heart. And its eyes winked milkily when it blinked. And
sometimes it had cawed in his ear and frightened him
awake. And you could feel its heart. But no longer.

Furian got up, and went out. He checked the palace
cautiously, knife in hand. No one was in the lower rooms.
Bony pallet beds lurked in upper chambers. Also a
chamber pot, months unemptied, was growing a curious
fern. He did up the window he had forced.

Why had del Nero's mask had such value it must be
traced, stolen back, killed for?

When he went up again, Shaachen was just the
same.

"I'll bury him," Shaachen said, "I've a big casket.
His little bones. I'll keep his bones. But they won't fly.
They won't tell me the time. Darling," he said to his
dead. "Darling."

Furian sat on a chair that had not been destroyed.
He felt sick and weary. Later it might be feasible to lead
the old man somewhere so he could rest.

He must have dozed, perhaps only a few minutes.

When he woke, there was a different noise in the
room.

"Hark," Shaachen whispered. "Do you hear?"

Furian heard. It was the sound of wings, fluttering, over the room, up and down. The magpie had come alive.

"No," said Shaachen, as if Furian had spoken aloud.

Something flew over the window. It might have been a trick of fever-sight. Then came a light knock on the table, a slight dripping.

"He knocks over my inkwell," said Shaachen. His voice was light and breathless and young. "Always he does it."

Something scraped, scraped.

Furian half moved. Shaachen hissed, "*Stay still*."

The scraping ceased.

A flurry of wings beat up, up into the ceiling, and stopped in midair.

They sat motionless for some minutes.

Then Shaachen came to his feet. He went to a candle-stub, and lit it. Walking to the desk, he laid the candle and the dead magpie down there. "Look, Furian, you see?"

Furian got up. He crossed to the desk. On one of the papers a message had been untidily written, black on white, as if by the unwieldy scraping of a beak dipped in spilled ink.

"Thus," said Shaachen. He rubbed his face. Perhaps it was only magic, though he had seemed too feeble. Shaachen said, "The body is the mask of the soul. Eh, darling?"

On the paper were the words: *Don't cry. I live*.

# PART TWO

# The Face

# 1

DID THE FALLEN ANGELS REMEMBER their time in the house of their father, God, with shamed nostalgia? Had they been happy then?

The last day of his happiness in his father's house had been soon after Furian's eighteenth birthday. It was, in memory, a canary yellow autumn. His family had been at the estate for two months, and he had just left the University of Venus, and come there, along the dusty roads, to be with them. What a party they gave him. He could still taste, six years later, the meats and wines, the crystallized pale oranges in shells of rich, saccharine black dolche. He could see the fireworks let off beyond the terrace, showers of crystal on the dark. His mother, his sister Caro, with sparkling eyes. And his father taking such proud tender pains to treat him as a man. "My son." The coat embroidered by butterflies. Music.

At dinner, was his father's favorite agent, who had docked in Venus not seven days before. Lepidus was a gentleman, much traveled, a show-piece conversational-ist. This time he had been as far as the Amarias, the mythical double continent dedicated to the Virgin.

Lepidus recounted his journey, after leaving ship at Candisi, and traveling overland. The trek had taken more than a year. He had seen broiling summers, and winters of such snows a man would sink and be lost in them as if in a lake. He had walked on rivers, and on the sea, iced ten feet deep. He saw the capital of Russa, with its core of metallic domes and green dragon-scale. Beyond, he crossed into the white land of Rus Parvus, Little Russa, (for it was Russa who had discovered the Amarias, two centuries before) traded for whale ivory figurines, the furs of bears, from the agate-eyed Argenti. Going south, by kayak and sled, he saw the great tent city of the tribal peoples named for brass, the Orichalci. One tribe now ruled the rest. They were called, in translation, plainly enough, The Enemy. They worshipped tribal gods, like the Argenti of the White Lands. They believed, too, all things had a physical soul, internal during life. the supernatural essence linked to yet separate from both body and spirit. They were a cruel and noble people, living more in an unseen world of magic and powers than on the plains and deserts of the continent. Here he might trade for tobacco from the long blue leaves the Orichalci smoked in their ritual pipes.

One more year, and Lepidus reached the ultimate south, the second Amaria. Here were drugs and jewels and gold, and the cobweb silk which would pass through a woman's ring. Also the wonderful dark sweetmeat, black dolche. This came from a little hard bean, just as coffee did.

The table sat entranced by Lepidus' stories. Furian recalled, his mother had asked, "But surely someone has gone by now to convert these poor heathen to the religion of the Christ?"

"Oh yes, Madama. But they don't take to it, especially in the north. Their belief in a certain type of spirit is so strong. Do you know, they beg the pardon of every beast they hunt, and bless and thank it after a kill? They fashion spears that resemble the beast, to show respect to it. They have ceremonies in the dark, dances with masks and manes of feather Every mask has the nature of some creature. They think all men are represented, on some higher corporeal plane, by a holy and non-physical part that yet is tied to the earth. The positions of the stars at birth, the nature of the man himself, these form his unseen psyche."

Furian's mother had turned uncomfortable, a touch ruffled. He could remember how he himself left an offering at the altar of Neptune in the City, minutes before he accepted divine communion at the altar of Christ.

"But can they comprehend the true soul?" asked Caro.

"Signorina, the soul to them is a stranger, something only to be regained with fleshly death. The *psyche* they constantly commune with while alive."

Furian's  mind had drifted. There was a lovely girl among the guests, the daughter of one of his father's friends. She was too old for him, twenty perhaps, but he had wondered if he might have some chance of something.

The evening ended after the fireworks.

On the pillared terrace, with its antique fountain, (a Hebe pouring water), Furian's mother came and took his hands. "My dear, my dear."

After the mother, the sister. "Are you really home now? Or will you go off at once to travel? Stay a little."

And then, only the last of the night. It was almost four o'clock.

The servants were going round the garden, putting out the paper lamps, the candles under colored glass.

A bird sang somewhere, perhaps from its cage, or in

the grounds, disturbed by all the lights.

His father's steward had approached, and said, "I'm glad to see you home, Signore."

"Thank you. So am I."

He had vowed to go out and visit the girl, and she had appeared to welcome this. She did not seem to mind the difference in their ages. She had allowed him, in the piecemeal shadows of a myrtle arbor, to stroke her upper breast, kiss the corner of her lips.

He looked up into the sky, where the stars were large and liquid, fixed and safe as diamonds on velvet.

Furian too might one day see the Amarias, and Russa. And he might begin to write the concerto. The first melody and the fugue had run in his mind all day. He knew himself happy. All his life after, he would recollect this fact. The sensation of happiness, full and warm. The past sound as a bell, the future gleaming beckoning before him, the present holding him in its steady safe hand.

He spoke a word of thanks to God, and crossed himself. And among the tress, a final lamp went out. Far off, the phantom of mountains had already an edge of bluish snow. It was the omen of a winter soon to come. He did not read it.

As he climbed the marble staircase, his hand on the gilded balustrade that showed fan-tailed birds—it was then. What had done it? The dying glimmers of the candelabra? The silence? The mystic last hour of departing night?

Between one step and the next. So swift.

Later, when he had tried to explain, they had said to him, all the ones he told, (the ones who shouted or pleaded, ranted, or mocked), that something must have occurred. Did he disremember? Had the lovely girl

spurned him? His father insulted him? Had he seen
something in the City which, only now, as night and ine-
briation perished, came back to him? But there was
nothing, no explicit, appalling thing. No petty upset. No
tragedy.

It was that he suddenly beheld, Here I am in this.
But this—*this*—

Furian had paused, in puzzlement. trying to think,
to think it out. It was elusive, ran before him, lashing its
tail. A fearful monster. Yet it led him on.

A servant below, seeing to the indoor candles, had
said, "Is there anything you want, Signore?"

"No—nothing, thank you."

And he climbed on, but the stair was a mountain
now, with blue snow on it, and a black elemental clung to
his back.

For the world was not this. The world was as he had
seen it. The stench of the beautiful canals. The divers'
children at Aquila and Silvia, their chests distended, and
all their bones showing. The beggars and the thieves.
The poor whores with draggled skirts and bare breasts
and star-shaped patches over their sores. Old men who
died. Young ones with knives. Children screaming in
pain and some too weak to cry at all. A starving dog. A
cat with a pigeon in its mouth. A drowned rat.

The world was trouble and hurt, age and decay and
death. And since hell was already in the world, small
chance it existed beyond it, or heaven either.

Furian felt and worried at these things as he
climbed the stair, which seemed to go on for miles.

In his room, he stood at a loss, gazing about him at
his rich man's possessions. They were no longer real. He
inhabited a fantasy.

He had thought, *Oh, I'm low tonight. It must be the*

*wine*. And he tried to go to bed cheerfully, clowning his drunkenness—stumbling, dropping things—which also was not real.

Almost as soon as he lay down, he slept. He dreamed a glamorous dream of walking through a garden, although not the garden of his father. The trees were made of Venusian glass. It was an hour after, and now he was wide awake. Presently he got up, and walked about.

Beyond the window and the balcony, a soft dawn wind was blowing up the Veneran plain. The sky was melting, and its lowest band was the color the fruits had been under the dolche.

If he tugged the rope, they too would get up and bring him a cup of hot black dolche, or a herbal tisane to help his slumbers.

He had only to ask, for all the doors to be opened to him.

But that was the fantasy again.

*This* was not life.

He sat on the balcony and watched the dawn flood up the sky like a blush. It was chilly. He shivered, but not from cold.

He was still reasoning with himself, and did not realize the days of lotuses were over.

All that morning he acted out his part, the performance of what he had, until the previous sunrise, been.

By noon his head ached and throbbed, and they indulged him, thinking he had got drunk at his party, and why not, why not.

He tried to write down the music that had been budding in his head. On the paper it looked as if it did not matter. Not because it was untuneful or inept, no, it was pleasing, gracious. But it was not real. The music of the real world was abrupt and sharpened, thorns without roses.

In two or three days he was sick. They called a physician who diagnosed a fever currently common in Venus, bred by her waters.

But when he had thrown the fever off, nothing had altered. The more he tried to push the being away, the being of reality, the worse it had hold of him. It was simpler to stop fighting.

He tried to tell Caro then. She did not grasp what he meant. At length, Furian approached his father.

"I need to go back there, I think. I need to live there. Not the way I did. In *their* way."

"Whose way, my son?"

Furian detailed the manner of real life. Poverty and lack, roughness and dis-grace.

His father laughed. His father told him Furian would do better to ride over to the estate of his father's friend. His father had heard a young lady there was pining for him.

Furian rode instead out into his own Father's estate. He watched the harvesters on the land. They were not, cared for by his God-fearing and generous family, so very wretched.

He found a wood, and stood bellowing at his father. Trying to vocalize the truth. But his father would never listen, or earnestly listening, would not hear.

Desperately, with a pang of horrible terror, Furian knew the abyss lay ready at his feet. And that he could only leap forward, into it.

# 2

Furian was dreaming. His father shouted at him. "Are you insane? What have I bred?"

And Furian's mother wept, her countenance a mirror of tears. Which he seemed to clutch also in his hand, the looking-glass that had reflected so often her face.

The new lodging lay among the slums near Silvia. He had gone away, and left implications elsewhere that he might have run further. Then come back close to home, as home had been. Was all this necessary? There had been nothing sinister since the murder attempt. They had the mask, whoever they were. Might that be the end of it, if he kept low, showed them proper frightened respect?

Shaachen had refused to move his ground. He let Furian supply five roughs, and chose a couple more from his clinic. These were to be Shaachen's guard. He had mixed, from unspilled stores, medicine for Furian's fever, then been busy burying the magpie in the iron casket, talking to it, calmly and lightly. It had shown it was spiritually alive, and so the burial was only for the sake of honor.

Furian was not sure what he had seen was to be credited. But he *had* seen it.

After swallowing Shaachen's bitter brew, Furian felt worse, perhaps a sign of its curative value. Once he had laid his false trail, he got into the dirty, lousy room, lay on the pallet, and slept like death for three or four hours. His dreams woke him, and flashing lights across his vision that only dispersed when he opened his eyes and sat up.

Mid-afternoon was in the slit of window. The heat was a hot syrup, and gladsome flies danced in the air.

He went and shouted down the house. The girl brought him a ewer of water to wash in and some food he did not want, so ate. When he was ready, he called up the two fellows from the lower rooms. One had a silver earring and the mask of a pig. The other had only a whitish eye-mask. The pig was named appropriately Porco. The other one would not give even his nickname; invented one on the spot. "Call me Modest, Signore."

"I'm going out," said Furian. "You'll come."

"You've put on a nice coat, Signore," commented Porco. He ambled forward and fingered the sleeve the Jewish tailor had set with such pains. Furian slapped Porco off. Porco apologized.

"Three of these each," said Furian, showing the money. "More, if there's trouble."

"What if they kill you, these people?" asked the cautious, ugly Modest.

"Then you can take what you want. But I'll probably haunt you. It's your work to see I survive."

Porco crossed himself and made the trident sign to Neptune. "Don't joke about that, Signore. My brother's uncle was haunted just that way."

Modest swore. "When you're dead you're dead."

Furian thought of the magpie. He said, "Better hope so."

They went out.

Either Shaachen's drug, or the illness, made it seem to Furian as though he walked through thick clouds of liquid. How fitting here, in Venus. Between the dirty stooping shacks and sick tenements, came sudden vistas of the Laguna Silvia, inky green, with pieces of distant buildings seeming afloat on her like tiered ships. A city resting on water.

Whores squawked or cajoled them from balconies. This too had some relevance.

The satchel, with other things Shaachen had supplied, from secret drawers and places behind the wall, seemed heavy as a boulder.

They were rowed across, walked, walked.

Modest grumbled. He did not like this sort of exercise. Porco tried to cheer him up, telling him it was good for him, and perhaps the Signore would stop and let them all have some refreshment at a tavern.

Furian said he wanted them stony sober.

"One little glass, Signore."

"No."

When they reached west into the City, they saw, or Furian did, across the stretch of the Laguna Fulvia. There, before the Primo Suvio, the masses had, more than six centuries ago, gathered to hear their priests exhort them to set out and rescue Christendom in Venus-built ships. The First Cry to the crusades. But now the white dome also floated, confectionery.

Furian felt dizzy. He wanted a glass of wine as desperately as Porco.

He was not sure of the way, coming in this fashion, along the alleys and narrow streets. He recognized a side canal all at once, as if a veil fell from his eyes.

"Has anyone been interested in us?"

"No one. I kept my eye out. One slut followed us a couple of streets, to see if we were worth pinching from. But decided she'd better not when Modest polished his knife."

A wanderer was idling by the steps of a ruinous old house. The house lamp hung almost in the water, reflecting like a silver pear.

What time was it? The little clouds above the Primo had been daubed with honey.

"We'll take that boat. We come to a house with gates and a garden. You'll stay by the gates, and I go in."

*But do I?* he thought. *Who's to say?*

The wanderlier eyed them distrustfully. Porco took up the place of two persons, but lean Modest less than the place of one.

Furian sat further up. He had the familiar sensation of how easy it would be to drop back in the canal and let it conclude matters.

Having described the house, Furian asked the wanderlier if he knew it.

"No, Signore. Some palace."

THE SKY HAD THE QUALITY of the dense, almost brown, gilding inside the Primo dome. Sunset then, or nearly. The tethered boat bumped gently by the steps, and Porco and Modest had got out, and were standing against the ornate iron gates, polishing, both of them now, their knives.

"Stop that. Stand over there."

Offended, they went along the pavement, and stood in the shade of a huge old acacia that towered above the wall.

Furian jangled the bell on the gate. He waited, look-ing into the garden. Beer-colored shadows wove the trees together. There were wild roses, blue wisteria turn-ing now away from flowers to a russet autumn mantle. A slender path ran through, and there was a statue at its turn, a Pan playing the syrinx.

No one came. Furian rang the bell a second time.

To his right, above, in the pastry architecture of the house, the tall window with its lattice, seen sidelong. The window was opaque white, the others stood in a row, these shuttered tight. He had not noticed them before.

It was so dangerous to have come here he had not bothered. Of all the things he could have done, the chanciest, the least clever. They would not have expected it of him. Or had they?

If no one came, was no one here? Was he prepared to climb up the gate? With Porco's help he could get to the top. Could swing over and down in the garden.

But no, someone was coming. Out from the side of the house as if from a flat wing of scenery in the theater.

An old, grey-haired servant in a leather apron, with some keys.

"What is it? What do you want?"

Furian wore the good coat. He was clean and combed. He had on yet another mask, a plain black oval, the eyes cut out, and a chiseled nose, and lips that must be hinged up for food or drink.

"Is your lady at home?" said Furian.

The man, who had a well-made mask in the form of a cat, said, "My lady? Who do you mean?"

"The mistress of the house. Madama of the butter-fly mask. I don't want to name her. I wouldn't presume."

"If she were here," said the old man, "Why do you want her?"

"I have some things with me," said Furian clearly. "Things useful to her work. To enrich her beauty. To assist her in reading the fates of those she must deal with."

An ordinary harlot would be intrigued. Or uneasy. Furian added, because probably she was not an ordinary harlot, "I sang her a song last night. Perhaps she heard me. Go and tell her, and see what she says."

He slipped his hand through the bars of the gate, and held out the bright piece of money.

The old man took it without a word, and then instantly, shaking his keys, unlocked the gate.

"She said you'd come."

Furian thought distinctly, *Into the cage. Conceivably she has someone waiting.*

He felt a galvanic rush of fear, and of readiness. The fever made him reckless, or his life. He said, "You don't object if my men wait just there? I wouldn't suggest they come in. Unless I have need of them, of course. They're rather... boisterous."

The old man said nothing. Furian walked in at the gate which was locked behind him.

The shadows were heavy in the garden now. They rippled against his eyes and he wondered what they concealed. Then the servant led him inside and through a tall dark doorway, into the house of the blue whore.


AFTER ALL HE HAD SUNK in the lagoon, and through time also, for this was the water of Ve Nera, as it had been once, clear and cool.

Her sala had walls and floor of blue marble, mottled and clouded with richer and more transparent blues. At the four corners, high up, was a carved woman's head

and throat, a light cobalt blue powdered by gilt. Each
was subtly different, crowned with a diadem, her blue
tresses caught with fruits and leaves. One had a silver
crescent moon on her forehead, one a quartz star, one a
sun of pale amber, and one the magic emblem of Venus
herself, shaped in glimmering electrum.

There was very little furniture. A sofa, a desk, a few
chairs, but these were fine. Before the window hung a
sheer curtain of white silk from a rail. And before this
had had been placed a harpsichord. It was painted indigo, with a scattering of flowers in various ghostly, faded
tones. The keys twinkled the distilled and sinking sunlight.

She was not in the chamber, no one was, which gave
him leisure to look at it. There would be no way out save
the two slim doors, for the lattice of the window would
resist flesh and bone.

Looking at his reflection in the marble was like
standing on water. Had Cloudio del Nero died in this
luminous room?

The second door, as he had expected, opened. A
cat-masked girl stood aside, and the woman entered.

Her dress had loose sleeves, a long loose train. It
was a creamy flaxen color, a few shades whiter than her
hair. The hairstyle, like the dress, looked artless. Some
drawn up, most left lying shining on her breast, down
her back along the train. It was marvelous hair, but
streaked with sheeny darker strands that he took at first
for some affectation. But they were not. She had begun
to go grey, like her elderly servant.

Somehow this disturbed him. He recalled her
hands, noted them now. They were young. She was not
more than twenty, if so old.

Her mask today, like his, was plain. An alabaster

face, lovely enough in a soulless, unliving way. It covered all her features, but, as she moved across the floor, he saw again her eyes.

They were the most extraordinary, impossible, *brilliant* blue, breakingly blue, like some flower or gem.

"So generous, Madama, to let me in—"

But she held up her hand. She sat down at the desk, took up the pen, and wrote. He watched the white feather. Its motion was dreamlike. And when the servant girl glidingly brought him the paper to read, this too was like a peculiar dream.

But even the magpie had been able to write, after death.

The words said, *I do not talk. Ask what you wish. I will answer as I may.*

Furian laughed. "You astonish me, Madama. How novel. I'd better make my questions as entertaining as you yourself. Is it a game?"

She wrote. The girl went back, replaced the first paper, took the next paper, brought it.

*No game. You must be patient.*

He said, "You don't need this assistant, surely. If I come closer, I can read over your shoulder."

Naturally she would refuse.

No. She nodded to the girl, who went directly out.

He went up to the desk, but then she again held up her hand. She placed the paper before him. It said, *Stand there.* He was to be before her, not at her back. Furian bowed.

He said, carelessly, "In my satchel here, I have some wonderful things, cosmetics, unguents, some of them from the East. If you'd like to try any sample, in privacy, Madama—"

She wrote.

Upside down now he read the words, *Is this why you sang beneath my window?*

Furian smiled behind his mask. "To gain your attention, of course. How lucky that I succeeded. And I thought you'd like the song."

She wrote. *Why?*

"Why? Well, Madama. It was composed by a talented man. And, I thought, composed for you."

She raised her head. Through the white mask-face her eyes—her *eyes*. They stared into his unblinking, without one flicker. They were the color of the aquamarine glass in the Madonna window of the Primo. Or perhaps the forget-me-not pane above the shrine of Venus. They were like holes into the sky of some other world.

He held her gaze. It was too easy. She was well trained, for there was no innocence in her look. She might have been blind... or some creature that could draw out your soul by its stare.

He had the urge to glance away. Wanted to very much. But somehow could not now let go—

She lowered her head. The alien lamps were bent on her paper. She wrote, *The song was not for me.*

"Oh, lady. That's not what I heard. All Venus says the song was for you. And the poor fellow died. Did you know?" She wrote. He reached across and caught her hand. She had been foolish enough to let herself be alone with him. Her skin was cold, satiny. He smelled a perfume, something warm and shadowy, like the sunset hour. "Won't you talk to me instead, Madama. Tell me your name, maybe. The song doesn't say what it is."

She took her hand out of his. She wrote, *I do not speak. I indicate the song was not for me: not that it was not about me. The song was about me. My name is Eurydiche.*

"Do you care to know mine?" he said.

She wrote, as he had anticipated, *Furiano*.

"That isn't truly my name, Madama," he said. "Only what they call me."

She wrote, *It is a perfect name. You are full of desperate fury.*

He flinched, as if she had struck him. And, as if she had, wanted to strike at her in turn. He said, quietly, "If names are to be suitable, then, Madama, is it death to look back at you?"

She rose to her feet. The brow of her mask was level with the upper lip of his. She was slight as vapor, her waist looked small enough to fit between his clasped hands. Only her breasts were fuller, covered by a crossing of lace.

Simple to dash her to bits. Or push her down and stab her through with the alternative weapon of sex. But he did not want her. This damnable iciness that was a warmth, the chill fish that must swim in her pale azure blood

"Never provoke one who's furious, lady."

She leaned down and wrote swiftly. *You have the legend wrongly. The musician Orpheus went to fetch Eurydiche from the kingdom of the dead. but he looked back at her. which broke the laws of hell, and so he lost her, and she him.* (He noticed her head moved as she wrote, attending the pen.)

"I know I had the legend wrongly, Blueness. I thought it suited you better that way."

She looked up again one second at him. Her eyes flashed as they had that time in the darkness. They were phosphorescent, like the evil canals which had poisoned him. The eyes of a sorceress. But she was only a trull.

Then she wrote again. *We are not speaking, Signore Furian. Now, as you said, it is a game. Perhaps you will leave.*

"And someone is outside the door to help me along with a blade?"

She wrote, *No one like that is there. And your friends are ready by the gate.*

"Yes, it was wise of me to bring them, wasn't it. And I might also have friends among the police."

He turned and walked across the floor and everything tilted, as if he did indeed walk on water. He felt her eyes attached to him still by a long aquamarine cord.

He thought, *Let go, you trollop. I've not done with you yet. This isn't over. You send men down into nothingness. A Medusa whose glare turns them to rock, not a Eurydiche. But perhaps I have the Mirror of Venus to show you your own face and so kill you.*

He did not look round. He opened the sala door where he had come in, and no one was there but the old servant, to conduct him through the house, and out the gate, to Porco and Modest, fretting in the sunfall.

# 3

SAN FUMO WAS SMOKING like a chimney in hell.

The crematory fires were underlit a rotten rose. Even as he looked down, a lamplit funeral rowed out across Silvia to the Island.

It was showy, each black carven boat prowed by a black carven horse with nodding jet ostrich plumes. The 'Charons' dealt their poles. A drummer sounded for the oars-beat, as they did in the slave galleys. Women were weeping.

Furian turned and walked back to his new lodging.

On the stair, a boy handed him a letter.

"From whom?"

"An old chancer with a bald head."

The seal in the wax was a profile of the goddess Diana. It came from Doctor Dianus Shaachen.

Furian read the note by candlelight, sitting on his rickety pallet.

'Come just before midnight. I mean to try the Arts for an answer.'

The Arts meant alchemy, black magic perhaps. Furian would be strengthless against any supernatural aggressor. No, it was, he thought, that Shaachen liked to show off.

Why go? Shaachen might pay him for attendance, but he did not need the cash.

There was, though, nothing else to do, save sit here, or prowl about the City, cautious for assassins, his brain ticking with ideas about the blue-eyed woman.

He looked for Porco and Modest. Modest refused to be of use.

"He doesn't like walking," said Porco.

"And you?"

"My woman's cooking my supper."

Furian left them and went out alone. Nothing had occurred. Even in her house, nothing. An instinct, maybe only obvious common sense, told him they were holding off, to see what he would do. (But why?) In any case, Porco and Modest bored him.

Nevertheless, Furian had dressed in slum clothes, and wore a rag mask that covered eyes and nose.

He went on foot around Silvia—Modest would decidedly have been aggrieved—went on through the alleys and over the bridges. There was a large party at the Castello Barbaron. From the long windows flames pealed molten. Torches dazzled up and down the street. They were playing music.

Furian looked up at their lights, a wolf out on the dark plains of Venus.

It was nearly eleven before he reached Shaachen's quarter.

In a wine shop a swarthy eye-masked man watched Furian sullenly. When Furian got up, the man followed him out. By a canal, Furian turned and felled him without comment. The man lay sprawled. "Give me a penny. Just a penny. All I wanted." Furian threw a handful of bronze to him, and went on.

* * *

"COME IN AT ONCE. Stay to the room's edges."

Shaachen had showed him up by the dim dregs of one candle, but in his study things had been tidied. There were two toughs at the downstairs door, and Shaachen had assured Furian the others were about, one even on the roof.

The casket with the magpie stood on a cabinet. It was locked. It gleamed in the candle stutter, wriggling as if with life.

"You're to be my witness," said Shaachen.

"To what?"

"I would have done it with the mask, but they took that."

"You want to call Powers and inquire why del Nero died.'

"That too."

"You might have been wiser to have gone to ground, Doctor."

Shaachen was lighting more candles. They burned up everywhere, on shelves, tables, the corners of the floor. There would be plenty of light.

"Don't you smell it," said Shaachen, his not-recently shaved head tufted and bristly as the magpie's had been, "don't you sniff an element of pride?"

"Whose?"

"They might kill us, or not. They like someone to know what they did. How clever they've been. And the little people, tiny insects who can't cause trouble. To us, who'd listen? It's safe. They frighten us, then let us be. To *know* and admire, and tremble."

Furian nodded. "Perhaps. And who are they?"

"I know one thing. I surprise you—the old fool, what can he find out. Who would want del Nero dead?"

Furian waited. Shaachen only peered and poked at the open circle drawn on his tiled floor.

"He was a nobleman's son," said Furian. "But he became a fine musician and composed a tune the whole City started singing."

"Jealous, someone," said Shaachen.

"Yes, it could be. Some member of the Musicians' Guild, angry at a rich man having fame and success as well."

"Come in the circle."

"If I must."

"Better than to be outside. Things will go on outside."

Shaachen's paraphernalia lay within, jars, boxes, a stand with a book. Magic needed many props. Furian stood well clear of it all to let the Doctor work. The room already prickled with energies, and Furian's fingers seemed full of pins.

"How is the fever?"

"It's well. I'm bad."

"You look like the painting of a sick saint."

"Thank you."

"The one with arrows through his belly."

"*Thank* you."

"Take the medicine."

"I think I prefer the illness. The last thing you gave me was full of crushed flies."

"It worked," said Shaachen, which was true.

Furian kept to one side. The wine he had had helped to hold him fairly steady. The nausea was gone, he was only cold, with a dull hot coldness, and every candle had a fever halo.

Shaachen seemed cheerful, bustling. Now he took up a silver shaker, and shook it. Little bells sounded. He cast something powdery down and fire broke at intervals along the circle. Shaachen closed the circle with chalk.

He read out from the book on the stand a list of long, grotesque names. The tongue was now Latin, now perhaps Egyptian, now some scratching Eastern thing, now mere noises, clicks and gutturals, hisses.

You did not laugh. For all this idiocy would work.

One of the first things Shaachen had shown him, years back, was a frost-blue angel misting through the window. It had a fiery sword in one hand, a brazen apple in the other. It had gone out like a blown flame at Shaachen's command, but sent a sort of imp to bring what Shaachen requested, which that night was a vial of holy oil.

It had certainly been oil. If sacred, it was debatable.

During former rituals the magpie was shut into the bedroom. Safe in the casket, perhaps it watched, at last.

A bubbling sound had begun in the room's four corners. Up the south window and the wall went a shadow. Solidifying there was a gigantic tortoise. On its back, a translucent jade ball, in which was light.

North, Furian heard the rustle of the black feathers of a crow. West, he glimpsed the white crocodile, and East the curious beast with a rat's head and spraying down of tail. These were the room's four guardians.

Shaachen spoke a disjointed, partly-rhyming litany in Latin.

The guardians faded, and directly beyond the circle, on the widest space of the floor, the three Zodians of the City appeared in a glowing triangle.

Scorpio, the sea scorpion, gleaming bronze, under his black iron planet of Vulcan; Cancer, a genderless veiled human form, holding in its arms the moon pearl; Pisces, the smaller fish visible within the sea-green womb of the greater fish, balancing the emerald radiant of Neptune.

Shaachen cast out through the circle, in at the edge of the zodiacal triangle, a piece of parchment. On it had been written the name *Cloudio del Nero*. There was a rush as physical matter met the energy of the psychium. The paper flared up, took wing; It was a black butterfly. It fluttered fragile as two charred leaves, on the softly-flaming ground.

Slowly now, a girl's shape, wound in a blue mantle, with the star of Venus on her forehead, formed between the City Zodians. She walked on air, through shadowy pillars, and dissolved.

"There is a woman in it," said Shaachen.

"Didn't I tell you?"

But Shaachen held up his hand—as she had done, that very woman—for silence.

A wind blew through the columns that were noticeable only by their absence. It blew into the faces of the men in the circle. A hot, sulfurus and cindery wind, as if swept straight from San Fumo, the Isle of the Dead.

Furian covered his mouth and nose with one hand.

Shaachen stood braced, leering. He spoke another incomprehensible word.

A black animal shouldered up out of the wind. Its eyes were like wet lava. It had curved horns and a mane of spikes, six sparking hoofs, a dragging phallus capped with a barb.

"A beast of rage," said Shaachen.

Furian's body shuddered, separate from him.

And then, where the butterfly lay on the parchment, pinned flat now, motionless, the mask evolved, exactly as Furian had first seen it, in the wrung-out, lavender water darkness at the onset of dawn.

Its black false hair spread out from it, the curls pointed up with gilt. The spangle-rimmed eyes and classical god-like nose and mouth. From the lips ran a trickle of ichor, shining. From the eyes ran raindrop tears.

A horrible moaning lament involved and possessed the air. It was a distortion of the melody del Nero had fashioned, played upon white-hot nerves by needles of probing steel. Unbearable embers of notes scattered. The mask *bled*.

Gradually, as they watched, it split in two agonized segments, and out of it crawled worms with beaked and eating mouths.

The image was so tangibly foul, Furian felt himself choking on it. He turned his head, and as he did, a voice screamed through the chamber.

*"Crossed! Clogged! Unstitched! Undone!"*

A sound came also between Furian's teeth. He felt his body bending double. He wondered, with a last horrible cynicism, what would he do to the magic if he puked inside the sorcerous ring? And held himself together with a mental fist.

But the horror was over. The lights had danced up bright, and when he looked, all the swirling pictures had vanished.

Shaachen too seemed bleached. His nose was standing out like a horn-shell.

"Now you know everything," said Furian.

"Ah, no. Not yet," said Shaachen. "Thank God." He spoke a prayer, and some other murky filmy something lifted from the room and was gone. "Let us sit. Sit, sit. There's wine in the decanter under the cloth."

They broke the circle. It had crumbled a little, and portions had run like old white dye. But it had kept them safe.

Shaachen said, "Evil was worked. He wasn't murdered in the usual way. But murdered, murdered for sure. What was done leaves an echo that continues. The mask knows—"

"You told me this before," said Furian.

"The mask knows, for it was the one who made the mask that killed him."

"A mask maker," Furian said, slow and stupid. He coughed, and righted himself and poured the wine.

"The Guild," said Shaachen, staring away to the astral landscape of some incarnation not this one, a prophet on a mountain. "The Guild of Mask Makers. Or that elite group among them who makes such masks as the dark Apollo."

"Not jealousy then?"

"Jealousy and fury were its friends."

There was a stain on the tiles, deep, acid green; a strange burn that might, by morning, have faded.


ON THE GRIMY GRIM BED, Furian tossed and turned. He had twenty minutes sleep before the girl woke him, pulling his shoulder.

"Let go, you harpy. Damn you."

The sun he had seen rise was of course still low, the sky yellowish nacre. A charming day, for anyone who had slept.

"I'm to give you this," said the girl obstreperously.

He took the paper. Shaachen again? It seemed not. The writing was characterless and careful, the sort you could purchase from professional scribes at street corners.

*Go to Aquila, and see the sight.*

"Who gave you this?"

"The flayer's boy."

"Who gave it *him*?"

"I don't know." The girl flounced.

He turned her out.

He stripped and washed in old water, shaking with fever and the previous night. His head was hollow, and full of the resonance of some *thing* that had no sound. (The echo of evil Shaachen had detailed.) More medicine. It burned now like that mark on the floor.

He put on a clean shirt, the decent coat. The black eye-mask.

To go where the paper said was madness. So he would go. Go and admire and tremble. They could have had him any way. Killed him. Perhaps he really did not matter to them, except as something to toy with.

Porco was at breakfast, a fine one shared with none, not even the slattern who had cooked it. Chicken livers in saffron. (He had profited by Furian.)

"Come on."

"Ah—Signore—"

"Look. Yes, silver. You'll come."

"I will. May God, Heavenly Maria and Neptunus forgive you, Signore."


AQUILA WAS THE GREAT LAGOON. Beyond, you could see the ocean, in a curve like the smoky iris of a green-blue eye. But Aquila looked leaden, and on the water drifted broken pots, weed that had been netted in, and a dead octopus fishermen were hauling to their hungry boats.

On the shores, and slid on platforms into the water, the buildings were picturesque in their depravity. Barnacles re-enameled the scaling walls. Everything but the lagoon had a green tinge. Even the sun.

Under Aquila lay the church of Maria Maka Selena. A little before noon, when the sun passed over, you might see at low tides the tilted clock face, a hundred feet down, looking up into the sun's eye. Old silver-leaf, the figures of maidens, all green now, malachite girls under a peridot sun...

"Bear up, Signore."

"Shut up, Porco."

What was he here to see? Presumably he had to hang about, and while he did, someone might come up and stick a knife in his side. Years before, there had been a plague of glass daggers—which, snapped off at the hilt after the blow, left few clues. There was a song too, *A dagger of glass thrust through my heart*—

A song was coming from nearby. A rushed song. Too fast. Furian realized, it was del Nero's largo, played on an uncontrolled and squeaky violin, at a trot.

All the petals of its beauty screwed into those hurried meaningless phrases. As if to have it over.

"That's splendid, that is," said Porco. "They're all playing it that way now. It was a dreary old dirge before. Some fiddle-player from the Musician's Guild, he started it fast, they say. It's better. You want to have a smile, don't you." (Keep smiling, *I* do.)

Furian groped after this. He said, "Which fiddle-player?"

"Don't know, Signore. They're all one to me. Scrape out a tune. He's got a lovely mask, they said. As nice as any you see."

The green bubble sun winked. It was blindingly white.

On the Laguna Aquila there had started a commotion.

A big boat was pushing off, and on the deck a

106

woman shrieked, struggling to pull herself in two.

Furian focused on her sluggishly, unevenly. Her hair a tousled tortured fairish mass, and her clothing half ripped off her, so people on the quay were laughing and pointing at her now. Her sagging breasts were bare, and one long thin leg—she was a parody of allurement. Her hands had been tied, probably to prevent her wounding herself or another. He grasped where she was going in the guardianship of her black-tunic jailers. The Madhouse lay behind Aquila, against the sea wall.

Poor bitch. There were jewels hanging on her dress, and a sparkling chain. She had a beautiful mask too, still demurely fixed for Carnival over her shrilling, screeching features.

It was made of ivory, the mask. A fan, fretted, out of which partly emerged the outlines of a delicious face. It had dawn pink lips, sultry evening lids.

He knew her mask. The Principessa Messalina. At the Revels of Diana—she had leapt to the altar, tearing her dress in the same wild way—

She swayed, writhed. He thought of the worms.

Porco was jeering.

Furian said, "Her name's Messalina. For the Madhouse, presumably."

"Heard she ran half-naked in the church. Wanted to have the priest on the altar. And all the men after. Some thing about her namesake."

"Messalina had all Rome in a night. The old empress, that is."

Furian realized it was not Porco who had delivered this information.

"Is it the Princess Messalina?"

"Oh yes."

"What happened to her?"

"Gone mad," said the newcomer. He had an odd familiarity. A brown lower face, and scrawled lips. There was a bruise on his jaw.

"And why did she go mad?"

"Women," said the man. "They're all mad anyway. But I'll add, Signore, those pretty masks, the best ones—they're unlucky."

"In what way?"

"The composer who died—or who's missing and supposed dead—he had one of those masks. An Apollo or Bacchus. And she—that one down there—she had her special mask from the Guild. Last year, the last autumn Carnival, there was a prince, I forget his name, he had a mask of some dead king, and he stuck a knife in his throat one evening at dinner "

"Did he have cause?" said Furian gently. "Indigestion, perhaps." He knew the man. Furian had knocked him flat the night before, then thrown him coins.

"No cause. He was rich as Pluto, and he had a good-looking wife. Fancy boys, too. Unlucky, the masks."

"Unlucky for some," said Furian. He reached across and took the man by the crotch, very hard.

The swarthy half-face grew mottled.

"Tell me," said Furian, "who sent you here."

"No—one—you were rough last night. Then you paid. Will you—pay—now—?"

Furian twisted his hand and the man fell on the paving. People skirted him. Venus was callous, particularly during Carnival.

"Where are you going?" gabbled Porco.

"To a jolly place."

"You want me? It's—this walking—"

"Go and worship your chicken livers."

\* \* \*

THERE WAS A WATER-MILL in the canal. The water was curded like fleece, splintered like glass, then running in calm, humped waves.

The wanderlier cursed the mill. They bumped against the steps, with an iron-studded door directly above.

Furian got up to it and rapped with the brass mask knocker, which was in the shape of a twelve-rayed solar disk, with hollow eyes and snarling mouth.

A lackey came. He wore a mauve coat. He looked sidelong at Furian.

"You understand," said Furian, going past him with a slight collision into the passage beyond, "I'm here on someone else's business."

"This is the Guild House. Only the Guild comes here."

"But I'm in."

"You can go out again."

"Is that so?"

Furian was not amazed when the mauve menial called, and three strong men in dark leathers appeared along the passage.

"My master," said Furian, "will be disappointed."

"He must send in writing. A meeting may then be arranged."

"With whom?"

"The Master, or his Captains."

"That's warlike. Why's that?"

"These are the proper titles," said the lackey.

The strong men stood in a well-made fence.

Furian nodded lovingly. "We will write."

Outside he stood and grinned, on the narrow pavement. He did not know why he grinned.

The water wheel churned the water.

Somewhere there was a violin player who distorted the Song of Cloudio del Nero, and perhaps it was he who had aimed at him, from jealousy. And somewhere were the husband and the lover of ugly Messalina, who both might wish her gone. And elsewhere, one year back, a dead man who might have had countless enemies, each powerful enough evidently to write to the Mask Guild, to meet with the Guild's Master, or his Captain.

A mask was made for friend or lover, either as a gift, or because they were persuaded to take one. And as the artisan worked, he worked out too how to accomplish a death. A very clever death, by madness or suicide...

For such a mask, so wonderful, there would be many fittings, choices. Talk, probably, things let slip.

And from these things the artisan, who was also the assassin, devised their ends.

But Virgo was in it, was she not? Virgo with glittering Venus on her brow and clad in alien magpie blue.

. . . Was that a little movement? There, by the side of that house, where a slip ran through, one canal mating with another . . .

Furian walked, not so very quickly, along the pavement.

The Silk Market lay behind this place. He knew it well, how not, from long ago early days. There would be a crowd and obstacles, and they were not to be despised, at this moment, in the hand of God.

# 4

A COLUMN STOLEN FROM EGYPT dominated the Setapassa. It was crowned by a sphinx of black basalt, forty-three feet in the air. Below, the silks, velvets and brocades hung like sheets of water, sky and sun.

At the edge of the square, the lacemakers palazzo raised ornate stone arches that rivaled the lace. West lay the glove-makers' booths, and tiny caves of shops squirreled away along the side streets, everything tasseled and sequined as in some Eastern fairy tale.

Furian had no interest in the market. The crowd, made up mostly of the more valuable citizens, had some attraction.

He slipped among them, by the noble with two milk white dogs on leash, the woman in her litter, pointing, with a pale yellow glove, at cloth the color of decaying lightning.

There was indeed someone behind him. He could mark it, the slight tumble through the crowd that followed him.

He got close to a gambling table, under smoke-banners of gauze, paused as if to watch. When he looked up, the crowd moved at its own pace, unbroken, but there was a woman standing not two feet away.

Furian recognized the boy first, in his grey University garment, and the plain half-mask scholars were requested to wear. Then, she.

Her gown was black velvet today, perhaps rather hot. It had tourmaline buttons on the bodice in the image of scorpions. Her mask was a black lace fan. In the eyeholes, her dark, greedy, lovely eyes sprang from his.

"Why, *Signora*," he said.

The boy jumped. Calypso, Juseppi's widow, did not.

She said, very low, "Get away, Signore. It isn't safe for you."

"But wonderful for you. Juseppi must have put all his fares aside to buy you such a gown."

"I've got a new protector. What do you care? You didn't want me."

"Ah, Signora, I tore a hole in my breeches wanting you. But you're such a stinking leech. I didn't dare."

"Fire be on you," she spat, still low and throaty as a dove.

Then he saw them coming for him again, the tell-tale crowd pleating slightly to this side and that.

"Farewell, Gorgeous," he said. "May God bless you." *"Fry and die. And fry."*


THE LITTLE CAVES JOLTED BY, much faster now, for Furian strode at speed. They seemed full of monkeys, who called to him, and cunning paws fluttered things which shone.

Where was he? Not far from Fulvia now.

He glanced back.

They were a blot in the general mass, about five of them, shouldering on. They looked, it seemed, like any parcel of rough men with a pocket of money, out for a day's sport.

Here was another open place. Veils hung down smelling of the incense of the East. Furian brushed through them. A cat on a perch spat at him as Calypso had done.

Then he was up against a line of booths. The busy crowd swilled and rocked against him, and beyond lay a canal, and over there it broadened, with boats going up and down, two or three close to the bank.

An idea was forming in his mind. It might be the fever again, (which made everything ripple and churn, made the sequins crash with nearly vocal violence, made him want to laugh), but then, there were these women, this scorpion bitch in her velvet, taken up with some wealthy man directly over the coffin; and the other one. The other—

A hand clenched possessively on his arm. He had waited too long.

Furian turned, smiling under his half-mask, and saw a friendly deadly half-masked smile returning.

"Signore. Won't you come with us? Eh?"

Furian put his knife, (ready, although he had forgotten it), between this one's ribs. The man dropped leisurely, keeping his friendly look.

As Furian tried to step away, another hand snaked across his eyes. A snatch. The sun—

The day was all over Furian's face. He had been unmasked.

The lout guffawed. And two others shouted: "Face! Face!"

It was too late to grab back the covering. Furian saw a sea of masks turning like cannon mouths.

"Where is it?" thundered a man, one of the crowd, playful, threatening.

Another screamed "No excuses. He's a bare-faced liar."

Hands leaped on him. They had his coat, his flesh. Round his throat—

He twisted, thrust them off, danced, dived, came up through a welter of material and curses, and fled.

The crowd was now a boiling pot. Fingers, claws, feet and punches, blows—They whistled and hooted.

All the world of the Setapassa was after him. It was a crime to go unmasked at Carnival.

He ran, striking out, towards the bluish break of the canal.

The cry was up behind him: *Face! Face!*

Bodies pelted aside—sweat, scent, breath—they saw what he was—lawbreaker—tried to trip and bring down. At least to impede. And they were laughing. He was fair game for anyone.

Something hurt in his side—had someone knifed him? No, he would not be running—his lungs tore. The sun hit his forehead with the mark of Cain—

Two women, excited, grappled him—"He's a pretty one, no wonder he won't mask—" their hands prying, feeling—he pushed them off—

He reached the edge of the water. About nine men thumped into his back, chortling and swearing. "String him up with the silks. Apostasy! Bloody bugger—"

Furian plunged out from the pavement into the nearest boat, which reared and galloped under him. He shouted at the wanderlier—surly, backing off, wishing him in the Inferno—"Row me. *That* way. Two silver duccas—"

"Bare-face. Get out."

"Five. Do it."

"It's not fortunate. Stupid fucker—"

"Six—"

The men on the street were leaning down, light-

hearted murderous brawny arms. Furian pounded them
off. They came back. To use his blade now would mean
death anyway.

Behind the lethal merriment, he marked the
masked grins of the gang who had followed.

"Seven duccas. Or I swim."

The wanderlier slashed the tether away. Still buck-
ing, they spun out on to the canal.

Furian sat down and put his arm over his face.

The crowd cat-called and maligned him. There
were no other boats filled yet. There would be.

"I'll take you to the Lace Palace back door, over
there. No further. Show us your coins."

Furian flung them on the planks between the seats.
Hoofs of the few horses kept in Venus pounded through
his skull.

Another boat had drawn close to the pavement. A
knot of men dashed over into it, yelping their vigor. At
least three belonged to the following gang.

If the crowd took him now, he would be helpless,
and then, so simple for someone to cut him, slip away.
Even a romantic glass dagger—who would see until it
was too late? *The bastard's dead. Serve him right for going
unmasked. The punishment of the gods.*

These vulnerable, malnourished and pathetic people,
for whose misery he had thrown away his life. These
*scum*—

They passed under a bridge.

"No further. Get out. They'll hole my boat."

Above, the whey-pale palace with its lacy arches.
Beyond, an alley.

He left the boat and raced for it.

He was sure where he was going now. The only
place possible. He recollected that other walk, the neces-

sary waterway. He had a start on them. The alley twisted. They always did.

A woman on a balcony saw him and squalled, *"Face! Face!"* It ran from side to side over his head. Inside his head.

He stumbled, and a thin dog rushed from his path, snarling.

His heart was a stone, which beat.

AS HE RAN, HE RENT AWAY part of his shirt sleeve. Under the lea of a dripping wall, he cut two eyeholes, tried to tie it over his upper face, succeeded. It might last.

He identified these byways from instinct only.

He might be wrong.

The chase had seemed to draw off, but he was not sure for the buzzing and hammering of the forge in his head.

Another wanderer. Dipping . . . dipping alloy of . . . water.

"Where you want? Who after you?"

"Mask slipped," he panted, "an enemy."

The man accepted him, rowed off up the backwater.

Furian saw, near, far off, the mirror faces of the houses repeated, and, in the depths, Venusian weed that clung and floated like hair. The mermaid hair of Venera.

"City of Met Darkness," Furian said.

"What you say?"

"That turn there."

"That's a bad canal. Got bad reputation."

"I know. It's why I'm going there."

"Get out here and walk."

Furian dislodged himself from the second wanderer.

"Pay me, you bastard drunk."

Furian smiled and cast down some coins.

"Not enough."

"Enough to buy something to poison yourself."

To the ring of threats and maledictions, Furian swung on.

The pavement became so narrow he could slip over, and in. Did not want to quite yet.

He coughed. No blood. That was encouraging, and a surprise.

No pursuit either.

Meant to chase him here? Back to the source. Why oh why?

Pavement too narrow now to walk on. Into this alley. Round, and along. High stones, blind windows. Somewhere a woman sang in a thin, hateful voice. Not the Song. Some hymn to deaf God.

Back up from the alleys. There, across the widening strip of water. A garden behind iron gates. A window behind an iron lattice.

How to cross. A puzzle. No bridge, no boat, no wings to fly.

Furian looked at the canal. If he went into it he might not come up again. But there was no other way, and for this moment he did not care. He would care tomorrow, if he lived.

The canals had already done most of their worst to him.

He eased over and took the water with a curious liquid agility that he was much aware of, seeing himself from far above, swimming couthly, barely stirring the water, the ripples of juicy green spreading like carving in chalcedony. And already... the bank.

But he could not pull himself up now...yes, but he could. His muscles were made of white fire, and would do anything, and there was music in his head, the Song at last, going too quickly.

Up the bank—it was done. Now only the gate to scale. The Black Gate of the Blue Trollop.

He put his foot into the gate's mesh and climbed. Pain lanced through him. It did not belong to him. He had two tops of the gate in his hands, pods or acorns. He dragged himself again upwards. Somehow the garden was there, and he dropped over into it. He landed on his feet. The impact met the impact of the hammers in his head. For an instant there was nothing. Then he was there again.

Furian slung himself against the sideward door of the house. Once, twice. He kicked it, and the door gave way.

The old servant was running at him, cat-mask lopsided.

Furian stopped. He said, hearing himself, voice clear and sound as a bell, "Out of my way, old man."

The servant stopped, too. He whined, ridiculously, "One day you'll be old."

"If I am, old man, you'll be dead." Furian felt the water of Venus sliding like glass over his skin and soul. "But celebrate. One day, I'll be dead too."

He went past the old man, who allowed it.

Furian walked up the stairs. He felt light as air and pain did not count. Minute diamonds lit and went out across his eyes, but at the top, after a little, when he reached the door of the sala, they cleared.

He could hear a harpsichord. Probably only in his brain. He opened the door.

The room was just as before, a haven of blue. Yet set now, motionless, inside a pane of ice. The drift of white ice was at the window. There before it, the frozen harpsichord, and the figure seated, playing slowly, somehow without movement.

The notes dripped and rippled. Water notes. Had she not heard him? No, he was made of liquid. He was a ghost.

But so was she.

The pale hair with its lines of grey, he saw it, drip-rippling like the water and the water-notes, as her shoulders tensed and rested and tensed. Strange melody, without form, a wandering descent. It was very sad. It was a mist, and these crystalline uncurlings in the mist, a search for what might never be found, a loss that might never end, a question, offered over and over, unheard, unspoken.

He realized his makeshift sleeve-mask had come off in the canal. His hair hung wet-heavy round him, made of lead. Water shimmered along the floor. It had no aroma, only something faint, like burning leaves—he could smell burning—

He spoke to her clearly, as he had below.

"Here I am."

She left off playing, and the ice-pane cracked.

For a moment her head glimpsed about, he saw the line of her cheek, the insane blueness of one eye.

She wore a gown like that, also, deep, drowning blue.

"Won't you greet me, Madama. I came all this way. You could say I was herded here like a sheep. Where do you run when the City's on fire? Into the fire's heart."

She turned. All at once. One second he saw the back of her, and then the front of her.

He had noted already she was unmasked.

She made no attempt to hide her face.

Furian felt his blood rush down within him like a flight of comets.

Her face—

She was as white as white marble, and she had been carved from it. She was like the women at the room's corners. She was not alive.

In the perfection of her pallor, the blue eyes scorched. Large, unblinking, the color of ecstasy or exquisite pain.

She was so beautiful, so unconscionable, that she was terrible as the face of the moon. She was not real. She was truth that was not real. Reality that was not real.

She was not alive, yet she lived. Nothing of her moved. She was a statue. Medusa, *changed to stone*.

He must—he looked away. He saw the floor, and great circles of it were rising and splashing upwards, and as they did so, soft as a cloud, the ceiling came down.

Furian fell to his knees, then forward. He lay stretched on the blue marble at the feet of unliving life, unreal reality. But did not know it any more.

# 5

CANCER THE CRAB, its genderless human guise and smoky Eastern veil put aside, walked sideways through the sea. Scorpio the bronze warrior stood on a column. The two fishes played, revolving in esoteric patterns. Furian swam strongly, against the silken current. It stroked his face with coolness. Eventually, he would need to come up for air. Not yet. It was so pleasant here, the City seen only far above, through half a mile of water. One day, the ocean would cover all Venus. It would be like the Flood. Then the City would lie looking up, as he looked up. Safe under the sea for ever. Streets and domes, towers and squares. The boats grounded. The beautiful faces under green drifting layers, like a flowery paving of lilies, or masks. All struggle done. It would be marvelous to sleep here. But he had better go up, and breathe.

Furian surfaced slowly, without tumult.

The bed was hard and smooth. Under his cheek, the warm silk pillow, firm and ungiving, yet oddly *not* hard. And the current, still stroking, cool and rhythmic, his forehead and his face. There was a low floral scent.

He opened his eyes. He moved his hand, across the living firm pillow of skirt, and woman.

121

Furian knew at once. He was not amazed. As if it had been prearranged.

"How kind of you," he said. "You're too generous. I haven't even promised to pay you yet."

The scent was her young, fragrant body. Irresistible delights. He was in her lap. like a child that had fallen. She had been stroking his face, quietly.

But she stopped. A shame, he had liked it. Now what?

His muscles gathered themselves—and nothing happened. He lay just as before.

"It seems I can't move," he said.

Her gentle hand came down and touched his lips with one finger.

At her touch, one part of him did move after all. The uselessness and ribaldry of this made him laugh softly. He had not seen her face again, thank God.

A bell was ringing. It penetrated his head and every thing broke in shards and went floating down.

When he came to once more, a pair of men in comely cat masks were carrying him up a staircase. This struck him as very funny, and his laughter now was louder, and put him away again.

He dreamed he lay on the sea, over downed Venus, with the drowned faces staring up from below. But a fearful moon stared down. He could not escape its appalling beauty or the two glistening, unblinking eyes that gazed through it at him, like razors.

When he woke he was comfortable. Nothing mattered. Someone had put a drink to his lips, which was bitter but appropriate in some essential way. The taste perhaps of healing herbs remembered. Or else a toxic draught to see him off. He went. He was in the sky now. and Venus-Virgo lay below, a woman in a blue dress with blue hair, eyes closed.

\* \* \*

"HOW LONG HAVE I BEEN HERE?" he said to the girl, who might have been the servant he had seen before, or the slut from the slum, abruptly washed and in a proper gown.

"It was yesterday you came. You fainted in Madama's sala."

"I know," he said. (He had thought that was a dream, too.) "Anyone would, wouldn't they." She made a prancing motion. She would say nothing. Or would she? "She's very pretty, your mistress."

"Some think so," said the girl.

"What do you think?"

She blinked a glance at him. He was intensely aware of all the movement of her face, the constant flicks of the eyelids, wet slide of the eyeballs, quirks of her mouth, even the slight distension of her nostrils as she took air in and out.

Furian said, "I suppose you're used to her."

The girl snapped, "She's modest. She stays covered mostly. "

"And only goes out at Carnival, a few weeks in autumn or spring. When she can be masked."

The girl said, "You must drink all the water in the jug there. No food until tonight."

He thought, *I'll be gone by then.*

But after she left, he turned on his side, and slept like the dead.

IN THE EVENING HE WOKE, and knew where he was, and recalled what had been said. When he sat up, the room was quite steady. It was probably not the ministrations of this diabolic house, rather Shaachen's medicine bringing on a crisis, now successfully past.

He looked about. A cup of wine stood on the chest by the bed, and an apple with a knife, (they trusted him?) Across the dim room, which was an ample one, an enamel bath had been filled by water that steamed.

They had taken his garments, and he had slept adequately without his shirt, but there in the corner, absurd on a pedestal, was a suit of clothes the like of which he had not seen for six years.

Furian ate the apple without using the knife, but he might keep the knife. It was a poor thing, but could be useful. The wine was thin with fresh water. She must have a well here, and a good one.

He went and sat in the bath and laved himself with the warm water. Nearby was an attendant razor—trust indeed.

The girl came in on a knock as he stood shaving cautiously at the unlit mirror, naked. Of course, she would have seen him in the bed. She began lighting lamps.

"Are you mine with the rest?"

"*No*, Signore!" She flushed to her hairline above and between the cat's ears.

"Only she's the whore, then."

"She isn't!" cried the girl. "How dare you say so! She's been charitable to you."

"I wonder why."

The girl hung her head.

"When you're ready, you're to go to the room to the left of the corridor."

"Am I."

The girl bridled. She said, "There are strong men in this house. Be careful."

"You mean I can't leave here until I'm told I may. You mean I can't have any of you until I pay."

The girl picked up a shoe from beside the suit on the pedestal. She flung it at him, but a little short. For a slave, she made free. But then, she thought nothing of him.

He said, "All right. I'll be obedient. Don't be cruel to me. You were so charming when I was sick."

"I was not," she rasped. "*She* was."

"Tell me why," he said.

"Why do you think?"

Confounded, Furian stared at her. Though she was masked and he not, he could see the blush again on her forehead. It was deep.

He said, "You think she likes me."

The girl lowered her head. She made an angry gesture. "*Yes.*"

"I'm flattered. But bemused. Why should she?"

"Who knows why one likes another one?" said the girl. Then, "She's been fair to me, all my life. You don't know her, I won't talk to you any more."

And she *ran* from the room, slamming the door.

Furian put down the razor. He walked to the small window, which he had already examined. Through the half open shutters, he looked out at the canal, but did not see it.

A new game? He thought of the delicacy of her soothing hand, the way she had drawn him in on her blue beach.

He thought of her face.

Furian cursed her.

But she had been cursed already.

Presently he put on the fine-spun shirt and linen, the elegant breeches and satin coat, the stockings and the buckled shoes. His hair, rinsed of the canal, he left as it was, for there was nothing to tie it with. And no mask.

He drank the last of the watered wine. He wanted something stronger, for now, presumably, he must go and stand there in a room with her again.

If she would have the decency to mask herself he did not know.

His own hands in the embroidered cuffs, (the nails so clean), reminded him of his father's house. His youth.

But nothing, not even memory, could come between him and her. Nothing at all.


IT WAS A SMALL, GRACIOUS ROOM, the walls brocaded in watered primrose, the ceiling high, and painted with cloud-blown gods.

They—or he—was to dine. At one end of the short table, the silver knives, a fork with a pearl set in the handle three goblets, two with stars, one of dull violet glass that held the candlelight in a single damson drop.

At the other end of the table, the ink, the quill, some sheets of paper.

There was a decanter too, and he filled his first glass, turning it almost black. Then drained it, and filled it again.

When she came in, he must thank her. For although it almost certainly *was* a game, it might not be the game he had thought. Perhaps she had loved del Nero, after all. Perhaps del Nero had been as petrified—strange, apt, horrible word—as Furian. The Song, an apology not a lament. Why then a murder?

The door, with its brocade panels, was opened.

Eurydiche came in through it.

She had on white this evening, the bodice sprinkled by little brilliants. Her breasts nestled above like doves. Her hair was powdered with silver, piled up, one long tress curling down and down.

She wore the plain white mask.

He bowed to her. He said, "You've been a saint to me, Madama. I didn't deserve it, naturally. But the saints, I understand, are always impartial."

She stood, looking at him. Through the eyeholes, her scalding eyes. He held them. Waited.

She went to the table, seated herself, and wrote. She pushed the paper to his place opposite. Her wrist was so slender, ringed by topazes, to match the room?

He too must go to the table. He picked up the paper. It read:

*Will you permit me to remove my mask? Can you bear it?*

For a moment he felt the dizzy weakness threaten him. He said, "I'm at your mercy, lady."

She wrote.

The paper came over the slight width of the table. (Seated, they would not be much more than four feet apart.)

He read the paper.

*That is not what I wish.*

He said, "Then I must leave."

She wrote. *You are not a captive. You were not stayed before. You returned here.*

"I was *driven* here, I think. Why?"

She raised her head.

He had a sudden ghastly desire to see it again, the carven slender moon of her face. He filled the glass. He said, "Take the thing off. You're discourteous to me, you didn't give me a mask."

She sat quite still. Then her hands went up, weightless. She undid hidden clasps, and let down the mask's inert poreless camouflage from the inert poreless mask beneath.

For her *face* was a mask.

She bowed her head again, and wrote. It took a little space. Then she pushed the paper with her fingertips and he took it up.

*You saw at once. Not everyone has done so. I will never grow old, at least, I will not seem to. Do not be afraid of my eyes. The phosphorescent look of them is from the distillation I must use to bathe them in. I never blink, they are never refreshed except from a little bottle I have. I cannot eat, only absorb liquid, that from a special vial. Of course, I would not let you see this. Please sit down, and be at ease. This thing you behold does not make me wicked. Imagine if you will, I am here behind this face, smiling, wishing to speak, and to listen.*

An uneven pulse throbbed through him. He looked at her. It was like looking at the sculpture of the most beautiful, or the face of the most beautiful who had died. She was made of stone. She was perfect. Her eyes did not blink, her lips did not part. The breath that was sucked in and out came by the effort of the lungs and throat. No doubt she would pour the liquid food into her throat, and the muscles there, able to work as those of the face did not, would carry the prescribed sustenance into her.

She could never be spoiled, it was true. No ugly frown or grimace or stupid amusement would ever mar her. The scars and wrinkles that perpetual expression made upon a face with age, could never come.

He raised his glass.

"I never saw anyone so beautiful." He drank. "A million women would envy you, Madama."

She wrote—it was her last page.

*Envy me that a man faints at the sight of me? Envy me that I can never laugh or cry, or close my eyes, even when sleeping? Call me Eurydiche. I like to hear my name. Few others ever say it.*

Furian said, "Surely Cloudio del Nero said your name? He's under the canal. The princess he couldn't make smile—why did you kill him? Was he unwilling?"

She stood up.

Her face and eyes burned with lunar nothingness. But her whole body was on fire with mute, trammeled emotion.

It startled him.

She made a beckoning gesture.

He saw it was the papers she wanted back, to go on writing.

Furian picked them up. He held them and said, "But, my dear, I don't know how much of this I can stand."

She came about the table, with the pen in her hand like a dagger.

Emotionless—in ferment. He felt the passion in her like the held-back vortex of some colossal tidal storm. She seized his hand and wrote across the palm in the uneven ink: *I cry. I live.*

They were almost the words of the magpie.

She let him go, and stood, flaming, empty, brimmed. Yet even her breasts did not move quickly with her breath. She could not breathe as she needed to. She turned away from him and caught the table and let go.

Then, after a moment, she walked silently across the room. She went into a corner where a marble goddess stood upright in the shadow.

She stood beside the goddess, and let him see, how alike they were. (How different?)

Furian said, "I don't want to distress you. Show me I misjudged you. There's darkness all round you. Will you talk about that? This isn't the time for courtly conversations."

She came back over the room. Her step was brisk. She seized a page out of his hands, took it to the ink well, dipped her pen and wrote.

She left the page lying.

"Wait—"

But she was gone out of the doors.

Furian bent to the paper.

*Eat what you wish. Leave my house when you wish. I will die of shame for trusting you.*

He turned when the door opened again. But it was the dinner coming in, silver trays and salvers, and the jewels of wines.

He watched them place the dishes, fill his plate, pour out the first mellifluous alcohol.

When it was all done, he sent them away.

He sat in the chair as the food went cold, reading over her words. He read the words on his hand, too, which, from closing it, had copied themselves in reflection. *I cry. I live.*


THERE WAS A WATER CLOCK in the room, over in another corner. The soft dripping he mistook for the canal, while a gilded galleon rode up a stem, and at what must be midnight, its top mast struck a tiny bell.

Furian had been drinking the purple wine from the purple glass. He had not taken very much, because the wine was good. All the lamps were guttering.

The door opened. The girl came in. Even her cat mask seemed swollen and moody. She put a parchment before him on the table, turned and went out with slapping skirts.

Furian picked up the new paper.

'Signore Furian, you are aware I know the name by

which you are called. Also I was informed you are no common adventurer, but the son of a respectable and powerful man. How am I cognizant of these things? There is one person to tell me. Let us leave that for the moment.

'I have few dealings with the City or the world. You will guess why. But Cloudio del Nero was my lover. I met him in a strange, unwanted way, but he took a great interest in me, and even offered me a secret marriage. I was fond of him, but no more, and did not agree. If he has died, I do not know the means, or even if it is so. Perhaps you will believe me. And that I am sorry.

'This I do comprehend, though not the reason: You are in mortal danger. You must trust me this much, while you remain in my house I may protect you. I was too proud before. I ask you now to remain a day or so, until perhaps your friends, or your estranged father, may be brought to assist you. I vow that you need not once see me while you are in the house, only my servants, who will go about your errands as is necessary, in order to invite aid.

'Forgive my former unwise words. Accept my help, and forget me.

—*Eurydiche*'.


At the bottom of the paper she had written an after thought, very small. *It is hard for me to act well in the human world. I was born as you see me, a freak. I have no measure, but expect nothing.*

Furian did see her, but as a child in a white dress, her face an ivory doll's face. She could not cry, save in her heart and mind.

He screwed up the paper and tossed it down. He went to the door, opened it. The corridor was in darkness, but for one other door at its opposite end, which stood an inch or two ajar. A mild light hung there, straight and still as a wand of magic.

Furian moved towards the door. He stopped and rapped on it quietly.

He heard the stir of a dress, pushed wide the door, and stepped in.

Eurydiche stood all across the room, which was her bedchamber. The bed had ebony posts, a painted lid, long drifted curtains. Candles burned on a table, where she had been writing. He shut the door.

Her back was to him, and as he took another step, she held up her hand, and the topazes on her wrist blinked as her gemstone eyes could not. *No closer.*

Her hair was undone, but the powder in it yet, so it glittered eerily as a moonlit wave.

"We'll say I did misjudge you, then," he said. "Why do you want to help me?" He stood looking at her back. She did nothing, and then she shook her head. Even she might say Yes, and No. "Your maid," he said, "thinks you fancy me." As he spoke the words a shower of brilliant lust went through him, but he felt again the draining weakness the illness had brought. Two disparate pangs.

He did not want her. So might have her. Yet also he wanted her as he had seldom desired a woman. For she was all the beauty and the misery of the world in one. Horror and pleasure, punishment and redemption.

And she? She could not say a word.

He walked over the room softly, but she detected him, and whirled about. *Her face—*

Furian came up against her, so her body met with his. He put his hands—the fine hands of his youth—on either side of the slender ivory disk. Her skin was firm and silken, cool as the autumn morning.

He leaned to her slowly, looking at her, into her death-blue eyes. His shadow put them out. His mouth was on hers.

Eurydiche did not push him away. She did not struggle.

He kissed her very lightly. She tasted of distant wine and cold fruits.

Furian drew back. "You can show me yes or no. Is it Yes?"

She put back her head on the slim pillar of her throat.

Her eyes blazed on his. Her head went up and down. *Yes*.

Furian took hold of her. He ran his arm behind her neck and put his mouth on hers again. It was possible to enter her mouth by a gentle pressure. She was lucid and sweet to the taste, her teeth unflawed and her tongue smooth and pliant, but moving only at the insistence of his own.

In the seconds when this utter laxness excited him to an unbearable pitch that might be the preface to aversion, her arms roped round his back. She gripped him, the coat, his hair, and her body gave way. Her weight was slight but he took all of it. She was heavy as a sleeping cat might be, a swathe of velvet. He picked her up off the floor and laid her on the bed. She would not let go of him. She pulled him back like a mermaid, intent on drowning, smothering him, drawing him down to the depths of the sea.

Beyond the room was the earth.

They spun in this microcosm, like a planet.

He brought her from her wrappings, thrust off his clothes. The garments lay tangled on the floor, like scraps of paper.

Finding her body, his desire now caused him pain. As she clung to him, her hands straying, clasping, he saw above the landscape of her flesh the visiting moon of her face. The face absorbed him. He returned to it, from her cupped breasts with their petal tips, from her flat soft belly, the pearls of her hip-bones, the tender feet with nails like shells, from the core of her with its rough fine pale amber hair, that did not match the greying flaxen of her head. He returned to her face, her beautiful resist-less mouth, kissing her, kissing her, eating her tongue, devouring her narrow cheekbones and the silver lashes of her windowed eyes.

Of course, no change in her, nothing. Yet he heard the breath rasp now in her throat. Her limbs quivered. A stream of arousal lit her groin and the buds of her breasts pushed into his palms, on one of which the words had blurred, (*I live*). But the face was remote. The face *listened* high above their world of shivering and searching and straining on, above her hands which teased his sex, practiced and cunning, her fingers that fluttered on his spine like wings, and sought inside him, so he must lay her out, open her wide, crucify her on the bursting burning pin of his body.

As he worked within her, the room and next the City fell apart. He heard the rumble of buildings fallen in canals and the insurge of the ocean.

Her hands leapt and seized him. Then fell away, strengthless. He felt long spasms rushing in her loins, but her up-tilted face watched blindly, far away. From her throat came a sound. One sound. And beneath his chest her heart gurned, striving for air she could not take.

As the crisis left her, he saw the opacity beneath the corundum of her gaze. He knew, she was unconscious in his arms as he had been in hers, but could not stay for her, went down in her, down to the ocean floor, where upturned faces lay with starry eyes, deep, deep below the water.


THEY LAY HALF ENTWINED. The house creaked stilly. Far off a bell sounded for three, but he did not know which church had given it voice.

"Is this dangerous for you?" he said. "If you faint at the peak—have I hurt you?"

She caressed him, his check, neck, shoulder. Along all the line of him until he came erect again inside the silk snare of her hand. She shook her head and spread herself, abandoned, arching her back.

Their race was swifter. They dropped together. He could not have stopped, he thought, to save the life of either of them.

"Who told you about me?" he asked.

She pointed at the table, where all but one candle had gone out. The pen was there. They forgot the pen.

"Eurydiche," he said.

In the dark which came, he said it over and over.

When morning bloomed, a silver haze at the narrow window, he saw her again. He lay face to face with her, staring at her, in and in at her. It seemed to him he himself did not blink any more, but when he said this to her, she hit him lightly with the back of her hand. She would nip him with her fingers, tickle him, tease him. She had almost every ordinary playful sexual skill.

He kissed the wide lids of her eyes, described with his tongue her brows, nostrils, lips.

His kisses were like stains of crushed lilac flowers along her groin, her breasts.

Outside it rained.

Daytime noises disturbed Venus. The canal filled and slopped on the pavement. Bells rang miles away.

Someone brought food, and after she indicated this, pointing at his mouth and stomach, the door, gestures bizarre yet amusing, he went and brought it in. He ate, and she, taking up a little glass with a spout that reminded him of Shaachen's alembics, poured the contents through her lips and back into her upturned throat. There was nothing ungraceful in the procedure. It pleased him. He too did it with the cooling dolche, and laughed at her, saying she was not mysterious. But then he told her she was a mermaid, and Venus, and Virgo, the goddess of the zodiac.

She must have tasted the dolche from his mouth. He asked if she liked it. She nodded. He licked out the cup and gave her more. (He wondered if she had done these things with Cloudio del Nero. But she had been fond of del Nero. Furian she had wanted.)

They slept through the afternoon when the window was peach.

In the dusk, when the window was steel, she mounted him. He watched her, her breasts, the face of the moon, the eyes of the stars. She drew him to a pinnacle that made him cry aloud.

Afterwards she lay on top of him, the face against his hair.

Some deep melancholy of divine pleasure made him weep. She watched, and putting her finger to his tears, placed them just within her mouth.

Later he lay over her and killed her again, and himself. For he felt himself near death with her. A wild febrile strength, born from the fever, now took all of him away, and it did not matter. He did not think beyond the room. Time, although it passed in colors at the window, had ceased. Life had drawn aside, as, for the dead, it does.

WHEN HE WOKE IN THE MORNING she was gone, and he turned into the bed, breathing up her fragrance from the sheet.

He found the next paper folded on a tray of food the girl bought and set outside the door.

'My love, make yourself ready. Tonight we are to go away. Trust me with your safety.'

She had spoken of trust before. Did he trust her? No. Not at all. Trust had no part in it. He would have to do what she said.

He rolled out of the bed. When he was dressed, and had eaten, he went about her room. He took the sleeves and skirts of her dresses out of a closet and nuzzled them. He observed her mirror, which had reflected her. Beyond a few garments, some gems, combs, a book that lay on a table, the pen and paper, she had left little of herself. What could there be of her. He had found that. What she was. A kernel of pure, cool, rushing fire.

Soon he went out to look for her, and met the old servant in the corridor. The man stood foursquare. Disapproval? Fear?

"She's gone out. You must wait, Signore."

"Will you send someone with a letter for me?"

"If you wish, Signore."

He wrote to Shaachen rapidly at her table.

'Blue-eyed Virgo I found. The one you know of. All is well. Who cares? Be wary yourself. I will write more when I can.'

Then he added, 'The Madonna, whose face is made

of alabaster. Better speak some spell for me, or say some prayer. Amen.'

IT WAS DUSK. They had not lit the lamps.

As she came into the sala, he crossed the room, and took hold of her.

She was mantled in black, and masked—the butterfly.

"Take the mask off. Let me look at you."

She did as he said.

He covered her mouth with kisses. He tried to ease her back. He would have possessed her against the marble wall.

But Eurydiche gently pushed him away; she 'said' No, and he let go of her.

She put into his hand another paper. But he shook for a moment with desire, and would not read it. Then he carried it to the veiled, darkening window.

'Flavio will come in with a cloak and mask. Put these on. Will you trust me as I asked?'

"No," he said.

He looked at her and she was masked again. She made a little redundant graceful gesture.

"You don't believe I don't trust you? But you might be taking me to my death."

She advanced slowly to him, and slipped her arms about his ribs. Turning her head, she laid it on his breast. Then, looking up with her whole face, as she must, she put her hand over his racketing heart.

"It's not fear," he said. "Lust."

And she leaned against him once more, probably feeling the lust quite well in its lower station.

Finally the door opened again and a young male

servant entered. He too wore a black mantle and a plain black mask. The black cloak and eye-mask he carried he handed to Furian with a quick half bow. The sort of bow Furian had not received for years and did not want now.

"Where are we going?"

Flavio said nothing, only went out again. Eurydiche led Furian to the desk. She wrote quickly. *Where you will be safe. I think no one else can assist you—and I was given word.*

"By whom?"

She wrote *Wait*.

"If I won't."

Her hand flashed up, impotent and angry, and caught his arm. She squeezed his flesh harshly.

"All right," he said. "It's all right. I'm at your mercy. Have I said that before? You can kill me any time. You've made a love-fool of me."

She shook her head rapidly. Another woman would have laughed, cursed him, perhaps shed tears. He took her hand and kissed the palm and closed her fingers on the kiss. He put on the half-mask and the cloak.

The sala, when they left it, was lost in indigo darkness.

# 6

THERE WAS LITTLE LIGHT.

As they descended the palace, he saw the servants had not bothered with any of the lamps.

There were no sounds.

Her man, Flavio, went first, then she. Furian came last. It seemed to him they moved stealthily. And yet, too, the gloom and shut doors of the house led him strangely to infer that no one, any more, was there.

In a passageway below the rooms, he sensed the water of the canal. They were certainly under the paving now.

Presently there was a door which Flavio unlocked.

A flight of steps ran down, wide, shallow and damp. A smoke rose from them, and there was the stink of bad water. A trickling susurrous came on all sides and beneath was blackness.

By the stair a lamp hung on a hook. Flavio took it down and lit it. This seemed an accustomed procedure. The steps lit three by three as they descended, and Furian heard the canny rats of Venus skittering away below.

They were in a long tunnel. Arches ribbed it over, and a bluish fungus grew on some of them, giving off a useless lightless glow. Not only under the canal, down into the lagoon, perhaps.

They walked without a word.

Sometimes Furian glimpsed rats as they fled away. They were albinos. There began to be other tunnels, narrower than the main channel, branching off. All were ignored. It was a secret thoroughfare, old sumps and sewers that had dried out, or places made purposely for just such clandestine travel. Though he had heard of such things, Furian had formerly avoided them.

Then they turned at last into a broader stretch, and there were new  lamps hanging up at intervals, infused with a thin, green, fluttering glare.

This was a general walkway, for in a minute or so, two shadowy masked men came strolling up to them, and passed without a greeting on either side.

Later another went by, this one with a rat-white (masked) dog at his heels.

Other stairways now began to appear, and narrow tunnels that sloped straight up. Some were marked by signs. One of these tunnels Flavio chose. Its entry was marked by a distinctive emblem, a snarling sun of bronze with open eye-slots; a mask: the symbol of the Mask Makers Guild. Furian checked.

She had brought him *here*?

But she turned and beckoned him in her mute, eloquent way. And he—he was a love-fool. He would do what she wished.

He followed her, and the servant, up the tunnel.

A bold gleaming lantern hung from a lion-shaped hook. There was a stair, the stone kept clean and quite dry. Having climbed it, they reached a slit of door, only wide enough a woman slender as Eurydiche could go through without turning sideways on.

Flavio knocked at the panels. A man's voice came at once. "Whom does the night give up?"

"Seekers of the risen sun."

"Name yourselves."

"Madonna Eurydiche, her slave, and one companion."

The phrases had an antique quality. The first had been apparently a password. Now there was the sound of bolts drawn, and the curtailed little door swung in.

Flavio turned himself and went through, Eurydiche went after, and Furian, grimacing, after them.

It was a tiny chamber, fitting the door. Two lamps lit it, and a man stood in a black apron, on his head the fearsome visage and wig of some ancient monstrosity. The mask was excellent in its way, fanged and tusked. The eyepieces had black glass in them.

Furian anticipated more preamble, but the door's guardian merely indicated a second door.

"You're expected, Madama."

The second door was of a normal size, and beyond was a stone passage, lighted at intervals by naked torches. The City knew, the palace of the Mask Guild was very old. Another flight of steps, these broad and white, took them to a double door.

Without hindrance they went through.

Beyond lay the Guild hall.

Furian thought, *Why be modest? Display is power*.

The ceiling looked high as a sky. It was painted as one, a green sky of tempest shown in panels, with boiling clouds. A sun set in fulvous glory to one corner. At the opposite corner a moon rose in a flock of stars. Every one a faceted glass that dazzled and winked.

Pillars held up the sky-ceiling on capitals of silver acanthus leaves. The tops of the walls had a frieze of

Roman marble, centaurs carrying off maidens. There was also a chandelier, fragile as some ornate gigantic jewelry, budding with thirty or fifty candles, everyone ablaze. Everything reflected in a floor like water.

On the walls were a hundred or more masks. They resembled terrible unmarred faces, staring, with tongues out or pursed lips, with rays for hair and horns like the moon, the snouts of beasts, or the loud, dumb beauty of the damned.

They journeyed through the hall, over the reflecting floor, (minuscule figures), and went through another door, along another corridor, to a tapestried wall that had no door at all.

Flavio stepped aside. He settled into a small alcove, and sat down. He set his lamp on a table there, familiarly.

Eurydiche turned to Furian. She touched his lips softly with her fingers: *Be silent.*

Then she knocked three times and three times again on the wall.

There was a sigh of sound, and the tapestry quivered. The wall had moved aside behind it.

Imperiously now, it seemed to him, inimical and unknown the woman glided through without a glance. Furian walked after her.


DEATH, FURIAN THOUGHT. *A whole room of it.*

In the bright shine of candles on gilded stands, a background of dark green serpentine, and resting there in rows, the countless yellowed smiling skulls. Beneath a dark window, forty-seven skulls that were black, no longer smiling, their teeth all dropped out.

*My welcome?*

She did not seem at a loss. She stood before a big

man's shape, which was seated, almost idly, in a chair. But her hands had come out from her cloak. They darted over the air, describing various forms. And the man had also raised two hands, one with a black ring upon it, and did the same.

They—were *speaking* together. It was almost instantly plain. A language that did not need tongues or lips.

She must know him well, he her, for this to be between them.

His hands were not young, nor old. Strong, spread, callused workman's hands, with cuffs of silver lace, and a ring worthy of the Ducem.

His face was masked oddly, a circular plate of deep blue glass, cut with two eyeholes and a gash for the mouth, having a hooked and bulbous nose. Beyond, his hair was strictly tied and streaked by heavy grey. The eyes were dark and veined, long-lidded, the containing skin creased and sallow. The eyes and hair and hands of a man in late middle age.

Furian did nothing, standing attending on their unfathomable conversation.

The conversation stopped. She turned her butterfly face towards him, seemed hesitating. Then she moved away. A curtain hung down and she went by it into some other room.

The man spoke at once.

"You are Eurydiche's lover."

Furian was unnerved. The voice—there was something to it . . . did he know it?

"If I am, what are you to her?"

The man said, flatly, "Her father."

Furian replied, "That warns me to be wary."

"It should not. She's told me everything. Besides, I expected nothing else."

Indeed, the voice was familiar. It stirred up the past, long avenues and vistas of gardens and fine chambers.

"Then you'll expect to abuse me," said Furian, levelly.

"Why should I expect that? You were always one who took what he wanted. Even when you wanted *nothing*, you took that."

"You know me? How interesting."

"And you know me," said the man. He undid the fastenings of the mask. It came off in his large hand.

It was a lined, audacious face. A gentleman's face, an explorer's face, for the tracks about the eyes had been formed by seas and sun and vigil.

An instant scene formed fast about him. It was in Furian's father's house. The long table draped and laid for some dinner. The oranges in dolche, and the musicians playing a little diversion. *Who?*

"You don't remember me? I was of so little account."

It came.

"Lepidus," Furian said.

His father's agent and captain, the man who had traveled so many lands on his father's business, even as far as Rus Parvus and the Southern Amaria. The silk that passed through a ring—

Lepidus. Now here, a maker of masks, the father of the woman whose face *was* a mask—

"You seem to know it all," said Furian, "but I'm in the dark."

"Surely not so much. You went hunting murderers."

"I only found a mask on a canal."

"You found my daughter. Do you still think she killed him, the composer of the song?"

"No. It isn't in her to kill."

"You think not? Ah, but you're right. She can only kill with a look, my child, can't she?"

Furian said nothing.

Lepidus got up. He went to a table and poured wine into two goblets of clear Venusian glass.

"Choose which you want."

"You think I'll suspect poison.

"Won't you?"

"I'm defenseless here anyway."

"You trusted her to bring you here." Furian shrugged. He took one of the glasses and drank it down. Lepidus refilled it. "You drink that way now."

"You know everything about me."

"I know something about you. That you left your father's house on a whim. I was on my own little estate at the time, but I heard of it. Your father wrote to me. Now and then, I've come across you in the City. You didn't look up from the gutter you were so determinedly in, to see me."

"My father asked you to watch me, then."

"Something like that. But later, you went your own way. It was Juseppi, your wanderlier of that night, who spoke of you in connection with del Nero's mask."

"He was, I think, made to speak of me."

"Perhaps."

"And then I was to be killed. And then, I was *not* to be killed. I'll assume that, since I'm not dead."

"That's because Eurydiche likes you. And it seems that you in turn like her quite well."

"Del Nero seemed to like her."

"He loved her. But she had no true feeling for him."

"A strange motive for murder."

Lepidus said, "As you guessed he was murdered for another reason. Someone was jealous and wished him away. A musician, you'll understand."

"But you had him killed on this jealous musician's behalf."

"I, and others."

"You had him set upon and thrown in the canal."

"Nothing so crude. It was wonderfully subtly done."

"*How* was it done?"

Lepidus smiled, in the broad raconteur's fashion that long ago had enchanted the supper tables. "That's another story. We may come to it. But not yet."

"Have there been others your Guild—and you, Lepidus—killed?"

"You know as much."

"Name them. Number them."

"Oh, five or so. Seven or so. The names might mean nothing."

"Messalina is one?"

"Yes."

"But she's gone mad. She's beyond you."

"Never think that, Furian. Shall I call you Furian? Since you call yourself that now."

"Why do it—why murder? If not for yourself?"

Lepidus drank his wine. He said, "But it has also *been* for me. And for the others who do as I do—also for them. We have our personal reasons, rages, thorns, for wanting this power over others, the God-Power of life and death. To toy—as we've been toyed with. It's become—our art." He paused. He said, "Let me tell you something about myself. That night of your dainty party, when you came home to your father's house, when you were going to your bed, I was riding to my estate. I hadn't been back to it for thirteen years. This is often the plight of the dedicated traveler. On your father's ventures, and on my own, thirteen years away. I had a wife.

Of course, you didn't know. Why would you bother to know, I was only an occasional guest. But I hadn't seen her, you perceive, for thirteen years, or the daughter she had borne me in my absence. Yes, my wife sent letters to me. She praised the little girl, said she was pretty and quick. And I, like any guilty parent, returned them gifts and money. The night when I came home, I found no daughter at all. All those years my wife had kept her with the nuns of Santa Dolora. I could not at first get from her why."

Furian waited, but Lepidus was silent.

Furian said, "So you went to see."

"She was brought to my house. She came veiled over like a frosty flower."

"But you took off the veil."

Lepidus said, his voice no longer urbane, but rasping and very thick, "I didn't lose my senses, as you did. But I crossed myself. I babbled to the Virgin. I broke out in a white sweat and had to void my bowels. They call it Fachia Pietra—Stone Face. It happens now and then, in every several million, million human things. The muscles are dead in the face. They may be moved manually, or how else could they feed, but in no spontaneous way. It never changes."

"She told me this."

"Stone Face," said Lepidus. "My daughter. An only child, did I say? My wife hadn't given her even a name. The nuns christened her Maria, as they did every foundling girl. Then a number. Maria Una and Maria Dua, and my daughter was Maria Setta. But the other Marias were afraid of her."

"However, you took her in."

"Did I? No. I gave her to paid servants to bring up. But as a lady. She wasn't meant for a nun-house. In her first letter to me she wrote *Dearest Father, I am quite happy now.*"

Furian's belly turned like a snake. His heart twisted. He said only, "And the language you make with your hands?"

"I learnt it in the Amarias. I learnt it for entertainment. The Orichalci invented it, for the speechless among them. She mastered it quickly. She'll teach it to you."

"To me. Why to me?"

Lepidus leant forward. He was heavy now, a tree at the fullness of its growth, stiffening. An angry raging tree. "You have a choice, Furian. She needs a protector, a man of her own age. A lover, a husband. I'll give you this, if you want it."

"Del Nero wanted. He was a prince."

"I told you. She didn't want him."

"But me she wants."

"You spoke to her in some garden. You were masked. But from that moment. You sang under her window. You were playing the love-game even then, though you may not think so. And you came with her here."

"That was perhaps unwise."

"Or sensible. If you won't have her, you can still live. Either way, there's only one course for you."

"Which is?"

"To become an initiate of the guild. Once its oaths and terrors bind you, you're safe to me, and to my comrades."

"I see that. Then I must. I don't want to die."

"That's new. You seemed half to want death a long while."

"But now I'm enslaved of your daughter."

"You were always perverse," said Lepidus.

Furian thought, *Perverse to love her then, so he thinks, For he does not. He hates her. This is a duty or some earthly trial.* (I am quite happy.) *In God's sweet name—*

"Well then," said Lepidus, "take more wine. You'll dine among us tonight. The rite that will place you in the Guild is a difficult and savage one. You must be prepared."

*Trapped like a wasp in sugar. No way out. Not yet.*

"Whatever you say," said Furian.

*And he's pleased to see me so. Those days and nights at my father's table, my family like lords, and Lepidus our actor, performing his life risked so often only an enthralling tale. And I with my eye on some girl, not properly attending. He does like it so, this. The poor wasp in the sugar of his daughter's skirts.*

*And what has he seen, spying on me? Flat drunk, sick, playing with knives—the men I've killed myself, the women I've had, depths to which I've sunk—my bloody dreams—I am a worthy punishment, he judges, for this daughter who shamed him with her beautiful deformity.*

# 7

THE DINING CHAMBER WAS DARK. The somber silks were from the East, and sables hung from ceiling to floor. His father would have appreciated it.

On the table the vessels gleamed. There were clams in a honey and garlic sauce, greens from the farms, peacock roasted and dressed with their feathers, calves livers, a dish of the peculiar floury *Batata* from the Amarias.

Furian ate sparingly, just enough to confirm his (demanded?) respect.

Eurydiche sat to his left, her mask obscuring her, eating, of course, nothing.

There were five others.

Lepidus, the blue glass mask hinged up to his nose. Three further men sat about the table, dressed richly enough, satins, lace, wigs, pins and rings and earrings. Each of these wore only an eye-mask, two quite plain, as was Furian's, and one in the form of a gilt half moon. The fifth person was another woman, who sat beside Moon Mask. She wore a black velvet dress with decorations of tourmaline sea scorpions. Her mask was a fantasy of a black fan. Calypso?

She gave no sign she had met with Furian. Unlike Eurydiche, she filled her plate and goblet, yet did not shift her mask to eat. She was restless, moving and rustling in her chair. Now and then she reached for her silver fork, or the glass, left them lying.

Once she spoke, very low, to Moon Mask. "I must take it off."

"Do what you want, dear heart," he responded. "Why not, Let me feast on your loveliness with the food."

But she did not even then remove her mask. Her fingers tapped the fan and fell away.

Was it Furian she was afraid to reveal herself before? Did she recognize him? Had she been told the truth of anything? Whatever else, she had come a distance from Juseppi's Osiris death in pieces and the open sunny rooms of the Bertro Palace.

Lepidus smiled on and on, a short, graven smile. The candles made rivulets on the rust brocade of his coat, as if he had come out of water. But that was not he.

He had had, Furian thought, none of this aura—of weight, of biding malice—at the tables of long ago. Or had Furian only missed it?

The men talked in a sort of code. The dialogue had the same antique ring as the phrases employed at the entry below. It was another new language, from which the uninitiated was excluded. He could not follow, could not enter, though he might hear every word.

This too they did for him, he believed. To demonstrate the well-walled kingdom he was to try to enter. But he had been promised a rough passage. Acolytes of any guild underwent traditional rituals and ordeals, and were sworn not to speak of them. Enough leaked out to make one chary. But now there was no choice.

Unless he and she might escape. Was that possible? Eurydiche relied upon Lepidus, her father. She had had to. If Furian proposed they should mislead and evade him, would she attend, or be able to disobey?

"When we are midway up the mountain, the fire may be seen," said one of the plain eye-masks. (No names had been given, not even Furian's—but then, they would know of *him*.)

"A ram caught in a thicket," said another man, "We must praise God for the fairness of its eyes."

That was how the talk was. Furian did not really heed. Nothing was to be got from it.

Calypso put her hand on her glass again, and again withdrew it.

Did she know these men were the ones who had ordered Juseppi's death, had had him tortured, then cut into bits and sent her in a basket? She must know. How else had she met her swain?

"I can't," she said.

No one gave her attention.

The mask she wore, had worn in the Setapassa, was exceptional. Every tine of the fan was fluted by the lacquer of black lace. The eyeholes were in the shape of roses. Her eyes behind were opaque and wandering.

"Four ships came to harbor," said Lepidus. "Now a fifth ship comes. We honor it." And he bowed to Furian, ironically. But the other men at the table also bowed. Furian at a loss, bowed back.

*They like a clever dog. They want it to beg for the bones.*

Calypso rose suddenly. She pointed past Furian into the shadows of sables. "Something's there!"

Her eyes were wide in the mask now. Furian could see their whites were inflamed, as if she had been in smoke.

"Nothing's there. Sit down," said Moon Mask, offhandedly now.

"It's a monkey. I can see a  monkey."

"Sit down. There's no monkey."

Lepidus said, "Perhaps the ghost of some animal that haunts the room." He touched Calypso's arm. "The hour's late. Our friend may wish for his bed. There are things to do tomorrow."

The men got up. Each nodded to Furian as he passed him, going out. Calypso walked behind the moon-masked man. She drew her skirts in close, away from invisible things which ran along the floor.

The door did not quite shut. Lepidus said, "The man will show you to your apartment. A little cramped, I fear. Perhaps you're used to that nowadays."

"Perhaps."

"My daughter will go to her own room, which I keep for her here. You see, the proprieties must be observed under this roof."

Furian said, "The lady in the black dress—"

"Juseppi's woman. Yes?"

"She seemed uneasy."

"Of course she is. She's a coarse woman and not fitted to be here. But one of our number lays claim to her, for the time being."

The servant had come to the doorway with a light. Furian must evidently now go. He turned to Eurydiche, and took up her hand. It was cold. He must go, and leave her with her hating father, but again, no choice.

He leaned and kissed her hair. Her fragrance disturbed him utterly. So much license had been abounding. He had thought they would still share a bed. Lepidus took him to the door. He whispered, "At last, of them all, one you can rescue."

Outside in the corridor, the black-aproned man led him away, up a stair into a maze of twines and doors.

The room was certainly small, and bare. The bed was

hard and narrow. On a table lay a Bible bound in black leather and a Neptunium, the book of prayers to the god of the ocean. A silver cross hung on the wall. In each corner, high up, was the symbol of Venus, beside the trident.

A barred window looked squinting on to darkness, but he heard the race of the mill along the canal.

There was water in a decanter, but belatedly cautious, he did not drink it.

He sat on the hard bed. With her, he had slept as mortal things are said to sleep. Alone, he did not think that sleep would come, nor wish to court it.

Furian listened to the water-race. Below that sound, the noises of the Guild House were stifled.

Despite what had been said, they might come up here to murder him—it had been admitted, power over life, to *toy* with it, appeased them. Or they begin their initiation ritual in the midst of the night, merely to unhinge him.

Did she know how much Lepidus hated her, loathed her? Probably she thought it inevitable and natural that he should. Yet she was brim-full, a poured fountain, of love.

His eyes clouded with fruitless fatigue. He would have given anything to have her here. He must speak to her tomorrow, if there were a moment's space. They should be gone, Her father had seemed to say he killed to work out his rage at her, upon mankind, like an angry, maddened god. And had she never known?

HE DREAMED OF A GREEN SALT-SWAN swimming alone along a night lagoon. The walls of ruins stood up, not a light showing. The swan parted its mouth, and screamed like a woman inside his head.

Furian lurched off the bed. This fresh habit of sleeping—he had slept despite himself.

He flung the door open and stared out. Feet were running, up and up. They became a boy in a black apron and plain black mask.

"Signore—come—come—"

"What?" he said. He caught the boy's shoulder.

"The lady—she'll need you—" cried the boy.

"Which lady?"

"Madonna Eurydiche."

As they rushed downstairs, along the corridors, he thought that she could not scream, could make scarcely any noise. If he had truly heard it, perhaps it was not her?

The boy was pulling him into a room. All the while, the boy choked and muttered in fear. No sooner was Furian inside than the boy ran away.

All Furian could see at first was Eurydiche. She wore a long pale night-robe, and her hair was loose. Behind her, the things of a bedroom—it must be hers. A tapestry on the wall of Diana hunting with white hounds, shone oddly in the light of the lamp. He saw the tapestry was askew, and why. A man lay under it and had wrenched at it in falling, it seemed.

The man was Lepidus. Still in his glamorous rusty coat, the ring on his hand which somehow yet clutched the edge of the hunt... A big, able body, and the hair, undone now, streaming out, but its grey discolored.

Eurydiche stood with her hands loose at her sides. When he spoke her name, she moved at once. She came at him. He saw the unhidden disk of her fearsome loveliness, the glitter of her inhuman sapphire eyes. Then she was ripping at him, beating him, struggling.

He caught her, held her still.

"I know—I know. I heard you screaming. I can hear you weeping. I *know*, my love. I can hear."

At this she dropped against him. He held her as her body shook itself to quiet in his arms.

She would tell him presently, writing erratically at the small table, how she had woken at a little noise, and seen the lamp alight, and then seen—this. Her father's body under the tapestry, still dressed and jeweled, but the hair undone and stained with blood, and all the face, from the fore head to the chin, cut neatly away, skin and flesh, muscle and sinew, features, mouth, eyes, (brain), leaving only one more grinning, dull-white skull.

# PART THREE
# The Skull

# 1

"DON'T LEAVE ME," she cried, so desperately. "How can you leave me? Do you want to break my heart—kill me—how can you go—my son—my darling—"

Furian lifted himself out of sleep. He was not used to sleep, for years it had been so evasive. Eurydiche had taught him how to slumber again, and how to eat if he were hungry, and how to drink more for pleasure than excess—But the dreams. Could she have kept the dreams away?

He said aloud to the blank room, "I left you, Mother. I'm sorry. I expect you recovered."

Had she? He had never inquired. He had heard nothing of them. Presumably Lepidus had known, before he removed from their service to make masks, and murder. But Lepidus would have to be tongue-tied now.

The room was long and low, and nets hung from hooks. One brown candle burned. The mattress was on the floor, and verminous.

Was her chamber as gross? Possibly the one who had got them away had made sure it was not.

He would never have placed Moon-Mask in the role of savior, but that was the one who had come in, as he held Eurydiche in the long silence.

"It's treachery. Enemies everywhere. Who knows who struck him? But you two must get away at once."

"Very well."

"Not by your own means. You must do what I say. Or you'll die, and so may she."

They went down, cloaked, masked, two more of those secret wanderers by night for whom the slinking boats of Venus were named.

Moon-Mask did not go with them, only his three men, their leader masked like a bull, as dead Juseppi had once tried to be.

The boat stole between the dark stone curtains of the houses, over the stony mirror water. It was a journey of hours. At last they passed into the Laguna Silvia.

Furian became aware, by the turns they took, they were going among the haunts of the fishers, the Divers Quarter.

Nets hung from windows, in the dark like spider webs. The smell of fish was dense. On the tethering poles, Neptunes stood up, moving a little, some with Filmy pearls put into them. On the sides of houses, on broken shutters, the City Zodians were painted, Scorpio, Cancro, Pesci. From one greenishly lit window thin as a pin, a child's voice fluted out, singing long cadences, being taught to breathe even by night.

But sunrise was coming by the time the wanderer's oar went down. They tied up at a reeking, crumbling pile of tenements. The upper story craned over, and up into this they went.

In the large communal room, men and women clothed in rags and remnants, sat amid an early break-fast of wheat porridge and bubbling rice kettles, turned to stare at the refinery of a woman smelling of perfume and masked like a butterfly. A huge eel lay on the table, its head off, still quaking. Children played shrieking with the writhing tail, pitiless in a pitiless world.

For some reason it reminded him, true incongruity, of the Orichalci, in their city of tents. The ducal tribe known as The Enemy, who honored the beasts they killed and spoke a blessing and a prayer for them. In their wild ceremonies under enormous moons, naked but for their sacred masks and manes of feathers, they invoked a quarry and called it to dance soul to soul with them.

They were taken up a stair, and put into separate chambers.

For they were not to lodge together. It would not fit with the 'proprieties'. A man guarded Furian's door, and another probably hers. He realized, slow and stupid, cursing himself, they had become prisoners.

When a skinny diver boy, in a rag mask, with huge chest and vivid eyes, (a necklet of blue pearls over his torn shirt), brought in a dish of polenta, Furian offered money. The child—he was not more than ten—laughed. He had a wonderful laugh, rich and full from large, sound lungs.

"Barter here, Signore. A fish-head, or a treasure from the drowned palaces. That's all we like."

"There's money under Silvia," said Furian indolently. (He had none, anyway, it had been left with his old clothes at her house.)

"*Antique* coins, Signore. Duccas from three centuries ago. Capitas from the Ancient Romans. *Those* I'd take. But still not let you out. The Maskers are mighty. How would we dare go against them?"

"You know then it's the Mask Guild."

The boy flirted with his eyes, saying, unspeaking, *You are the dupe, not I.*

When the boy had gone, and Furian had eaten some of the porridge, he went to the slit of window and peered down. Outside was the building's back, an encrusted alley strung with shreds of washing.

The window was like a keyhole, too narrow to provide an exit. The drop anyway was some twenty-five feet.

He thought of Eurydiche. Was she mourning? Had her grief been for loss, or made more of terror, dislocation. Was she truly an innocent? How could she be. It was a fact, with her face she could never have misled him, by a false yet winning smile, an unreal expression of pain. But, conversely, she might hide it all.

Carnival. The word itself—farewell to the flesh that was, a practice for the grave.

He needed to speak to her, as best they could. He needed—to know . . .

There was an old beggar man coming down the alley, stooped over, his head bound in a dirty turban. He used a stick and had a scruffy satchel on his shoulder. There was something untidy, black and white, attached to the strap.

Furian could do nothing but wait. Maybe, if he asked to see her, it would be allowed. But no doubt, they would be observed.

He was half turning for the door, to speak to Moon-Mask's hireling outside, when he heard the beggar singing below. It was del Nero's song, rendered very horribly. Furian was at least able to tip the leavings of porridge on the old devil's head—

The man leered up. He wore for a mask a strip of cloth. His face was nearly black, and covered over with blemishes and warts. One bright eye like faceted glass glittered up into Furian's. The thing on his shoulder resolved itself. It had been preening, and was a magpie, smart as the most fashionable hat.

Furian stayed dead still.

The beggar reached into his satchel and brought out a little folded square of paper. He gave it to the bird, and pointed up. Furian heard the words, "There it is, darling."

The magpie shot straight up and landed in the narrow window. It was young and cream-smooth, and had the sheen on its feathers, unearthly blue. Its eye was sharper than the beggar's, like a sliver of black steel. It dropped the paper in the room, and Furian saw the words there, written on the back, *Ask him the time*.

Furian stared at the magpie. He said, "Tell me what time it is."

The bird cocked its shining head.

It cawed throatily eight times, without hesitating. Furian had heard the bell faintly from Santa Lala, not long before, sound the same number.

"What minutes?"

The magpie thought, raised its right wing to show a lapse after the hour, and pecked ten times.

Furian had the urge to touch the magpie, which had been dead, but was now alive in the flesh, doing its former trick. But as he stretched out his hand, the bird veered from the window and dived down again to the alley.

Furian pressed his face through the window.

"Shaachen?"

The old beggar—Shaachen in extravagant disguise —gave a cackle. He limped away along the alley, the magpie on his head.

Damn him to hell. Was this the hour for theater? Where in God's name was he off to?

Furian, with nothing else to do, picked up the folded paper. Opened it.

'Furian Furiano, you were not so difficult to find. I had one watch the Guild, and so by night he followed you. You are in deep now. I have not forsaken you. It is a plot thick as the best fish stew. Take note. The Principessa Messalina died today.'

Furian softly cursed. A glance showed him the rest of the paper was all about the magpie. He read, fretfully, how the bird had flown in at Shaachen's street door and upstairs. How it resembled the dead magpie in all ways, and could do, outright, all the same tricks, particularly the trick of time-telling.

The letter ended, piously, 'Consider this creature, and this sign. Fear nothing. The world is an illusion, and we may pull off the veil. Find you I will. Keep this letter.'

Furian sat down heavily on the uncertain stool. He put the letter into his coat, and started soundlessly laughing. Of all the things Shaachen might have done, he had chosen *this*. A demonstration of the afterlife and the miraculous recurrence of things. Rescue had obviously been too paltry, too normal an act to attempt.

Soon after, the door opened again. The Guild man in the bull mask walked in.

"These quarters are uncomfortable, but you need only suffer them until tonight."

"Where is *she*?" said Furian.

"The lady Eurydiche is safe."

"I should like to see the lady."

"She's occupied. At prayer for her father. Better not to disturb her. The priest is with her now."

"Oh yes?"

"Tonight we go over to the Isle. Lepidus will be buried in the Guild mausoleum."

"I see. And I?"

"Go with us. You're under the protection of the Signore Lunario."

Moon-Mask—probably the name was not his given one.

"We have a chapel on the Isle," said the bull-faced man, "There, the death of Lepidus will be examined."

Furian said, slowly, "You mean you'll hold your own trial? Nothing so banal as the Ducem's justice for the Guild."

"We exert certain rights upon our own."

"But I'm not your own."

"You were to be so."

"Am I suspected?" Furian said.

"You may say everyone of us is suspected, Signore. You, with the rest, were in the Guild House."

"Why would I kill Lepidus, my protector?"

"Who knows. Perhaps *you* know, Signore."

Furian held back his anger and the creeping coldness. "And she?"

"She was his child, Signore. She accompanies us, appropriately, to honor the funeral."

When Bull-Mask had gone out again, Furian sat down once more, and cursed Shaachen more thoroughly. But Shaachen might have had, after all, difficulties. The Mask Guild, like all the guilds, was powerful indeed, and in any case, Furian could not leave the girl alone among them. Despite what had just been said, she too had her motives for harming the manipulative and unkind father. To be despised did not make one generous, no matter what gifts of cash or security, even of common speech, were rendered in place of love. Besides, Lepidus was himself a murderer—and with a long reach. Even the Princess Messalina had not been safe in the Madhouse.

Had Eurydiche known all that? How not? She was not simple, she was not blind or deaf.

Tonight they would be taking her, whatever her guilt or blamelessness, will or aversion, ferrying her father's corpse across Silvia, to the Isle of the Dead.

AS THE LIGHTS OF THE CITY drew away, the bell was tolling from Santa Lala. Above, black gulls flew in silence, escorting the vessel.

It was a charon, a funeral ship. From stem to stern, a craft of forty feet, heavy in the water, painted for darkness and trimmed with brass stars. At the stern and at the prow, their pallid arms outstretched with gilded wreathes, stood two wooden angels of death in black robes, heads bowed under curving, brooding wings. Aft, the cabin, with its silvered tassels and marble-tinged drapes, where the coffin lay under black velvet.

There were three oarsmen, clad in the single black garment that dehumanized the body, and cloaked the head, leaving only the mask of a skull, its eyeholes blotted by somber glass.

This, for Lepidus, an omen extra. It had come to Furian, as he paced out the day, that he had heard of it before, this cutting away of the face of a man, the scorching out of his brain with hot iron, to leave only bone. It was a practice of the Orichalci, their means of slaying a dear foe. He had learned of it, at his father's house, and from the lips of Lepidus himself. That was not a dinner. Lepidus had been telling his traveler's tales in the inner garden. Furian, fourteen then, had halted to listen. He had thought the mode of murder had been described so fully for his sole benefit—the man kept glancing at him, gauging whether or not Furian was distressed or thrilled. And Furian had walked away.

But from the eventuality there had been no escape.

Eurydiche sat distantly from him in the charon, by the cabin with the box. Moon-Mask Lunario stood beside her.

They had brought her a black gown, a plain white mask. Her hair was garnished by silver powder and a string of opals.

She had not made any move toward Furian. Nor had he spoken to her. Masked, dumb, they had seen each other. Nothing else was possible.

The water of the lagoon seemed half solid, yet the oars moved in it without effort.

Trickles of the dim lamps of Venus ran alongside, next slipped behind. In another country, a fishing boat stole from the lost shore.

But ahead, the Island glared like a volcano on the water. Her crematoria were busy tonight. Although some miles in length, there was no room for all the City to lie there. Most must go into the fires, and accept a little bed, one foot square, for their ashes to rest in. Long, long ago, a special dispensation had come from Rome, promising that, on the Last Day, God would reassemble these fragments into wholeness, for what was God, but a great magician.

The Mask Guild had other means, the powerful usually did. A mausoleum, a chapel. Rich men, they said, sleep *long* on San Fumo.

The old-blood light began to make a path along the lagoon for the funeral barge to take.

*We are rowing towards hell.*

Furian tried to put the thought aside. *For all I know my father may be there. In a cramped merchant's tomb. buried upright. Buried, for all that. Or—Oh God—my mother—Caro—*

Thoughts wrung his mind. He pushed them off. He must think of her.

It seemed, he thought, they were at the middle of the lagoon. Venus was a curve about the water, two loving arms, dull-braceleted by lights. The Island—hell— lay ahead. And beyond, the sea wall, and so the sea.

It might—it *might* be feasible to get away. Some boat, the ocean. A galley, putting out for Candisi or the East, might take them aboard. His lush coat, her opals, payment. The galleys were wanton ships, rowed often by slaves, half lawless. He would need to bluff them in some way, but then, his life had been a bluff, until he came to her. To Eurydiche.

And the song: *Before you, darkness ruled me.*

He turned to her involuntarily. She sat like a doll. But Lunario Moon-Mask was picking over the deck towards him.

"Are you at ease, Signore?"

"No. But who would expect me to be?"

"I regret, in a few seconds you will be less easy than now."

Furian felt two pairs of hands seize him. Unsensible, he had been gaping only at her. But after all, there were ten men on the boat, and none his friend. While bloody insane Shaachen—

"Don't resist. If you upset the boat, *she* will go into the water. She doesn't swim. Did you know?"

He let them manhandle him. He looked again towards her.

The plain white mask was tilted to him. But that was all. No movement. No expostulation. Not even the glimpse of her uncanny blue eyes. She must have known.

As they stood him up, his feet tied at the ankles, and supported him carefully, and the boat, a very little, rocked, he thought, *A day and night of sexual pleasure. That was all she wanted. She had it. Now I'm meat for them.* And he said aloud, "Farewell to the flesh."

The last stooping man stood up. (Into the water once again.)

Lunario said, solicitously, "The weight he's tied to your feet will take you to the bottom. You'll see many interesting sights as you drown."

Furian said, "Choke on your own blood, fuck you, you thing."

As they hefted him high, he wanted to shout at her, but nothing could get up his throat but a taste of the mud to come.

Then the night wheeled over. The sky unshawled, and the City was in the sky. He hit the fire-pathed wet before he was ready. There were no prayers to say. He took one huge breath of air as he went down. For beneath the lagoon he must attempt to cut the lead weight from his feet—but he had not even brought with him the little apple knife. Not trusting her, he had trusted her. Love-fool—love—

Night and water and death closed over his head.

# 2

IT WAS SO COLD, THE WATER, so viscous and clinging. It was like despair. It probed him, his nose and ears, into his open eyes. He leaned to the weight to which his feet had been tied. As he fell, he took hold of it and wrestled with it. But the rope was strong and new, and the attachment was, as he had thought, a chunk of lead. Heavy as a hundred years it dragged him down, impervious to his struggles. His mask, dislodged, was gone. As his life soon would be.

There was no reason to fight. More philosophical to give up, take in draughts of the water, and die as thoroughly and swiftly as he was able.

But no. Lungs bursting now, he still tried to pick away the rope, to pull out his feet, shoes off in the water, kicking.

His sight was darkening. He could see nothing, only the silvery bubbles that were the last of his air.

And then the sea was alight, and out of the light, grey figures slid towards him.

Were these great fish from the outer ocean—the mythical serpent of the canals—come to devour him fresh?

In the panic of drowning, Furian now fought with

everything, the rope, the weight, the salt water of the lagoon, the hands that came and took him, and grasped his ankles, and forced over his head one enormous bubble of the wasted air. At his neck was a pulling, a tension.

He could not hold off any longer. His lungs rucked, spasmed, gasped, and the fluid rushed in.

But he could breathe the fluid. It smelled bad and had a color, which was a sort of fusty brown. But he could breathe it—his head cleared a little. How—

The hands let him go, he spun a brief way. His sight came back in green pulses. The light was green. He beheld a fantastic vision.

Three rag-masked divers, one a boy, the boy with the pearls, hung in the water close to him. The boy was grinning a shark's white teeth. They could hold their air, trained almost since birth to do so. The two men held up, in curious glass globes, oil torches that burned with a sea-green splutter. One of these globes—Furian touched it, disbelievingly—they had crushed down over his head. It had air in it, and kept it, the opening secured at his neck with a leather brace closed fast. The rope and lead had been cut from his feet.

One of the men made a spear-like pointing gesture.

They had saved his life. He was to follow them.

He did exactly as they commanded.


HE HAD DREAMED OF THIS, but not expected to see it awake: subaqueous Venus.

They had dropped further into the cup of the lagoon. The torch-men swam ahead, the boy after. Furian behind them.

Their lights lit first only the outer darkness of the water, formless, fathomless, secret. Fish came from it, and flared away, like crystals, like butterflies. Long curtains of weed trailed down, and through the weed they went, and things hung in the weed, God knew what, huge fish or octopus—they were amorphous specters, shining with their own soiled luminescence.

There began to be a sort of general glow. It was the phosphorous of the sea.

First he saw a tower appear, manifesting dim and beautiful as nothing seen on land. It had been a campanile, and in the filigree of its head he noted the tumbled bell, green as a bottle, chained with weed.

After the tower, they moved between high walls. Furian looked down into a square, the buildings partly fallen, but there was a line of arches, luminous and gilded, and there a column with a white sphinx, a pale sister to the sphinx of the Setapassa.

From ice-glassed windows, buckled lattices and balconies of black lace unrolled. The weed made banners, now turquoise blue, now glaucous green. A staircase shelved away, on every step some eccentric prize, a broken urn carved with goddesses, a pitcher of battered silver, a drowned boat, (a wanderer), with barnacles smothering her like lusterless gems.

They sailed through the upper story of a gutted palazzo. Below, were marble floors, Furian saw skulls down there, not lilies, not faces or masks, skulls looking up with wide open eyes.

The boy squirmed back and tugged at his arm, indicating upward.

They rose, the men, the boy and he, up by the spire of a coraline church, past its leaning cross, the gargoyles with weed-bearded fangs—even the Devil had drowned here.

One by one the men came up through the skin of

the lagoon. They were behind a small islet with fishing boats. The open water lay spread beyond. Across the surface, the stain of San Fumo's fires. There was no sign of the funeral barge.

One of the men undid the lacing of the leather brace, and lifted off Furian's globe. Its air was oven-hot and sour, and meeting the cleanness of the night, he coughed.

"We must go down again, Signore. For us it's nothing, but you needed to renew the breath in the globe."

"Thanks for my life," he said. "Why did you?"

The speaking man smiled. "You're all one to us, Signore, you're landsmen. Say perhaps we judged you weren't ready to die. Not in a state of grace."

The other laughed. The boy looked serious. He said, overriding the uncaring adults, a serious teacher, "Breathe much now, Signore. As though you drank when thirsty. It's another long swim."

He did as the boy told him, and when they put the globe over his head once more, the air smelled cool and clean and raised his spirits like good brandy. He was happy to descend again. He wanted to see more of the water City. He was alive. He had lost everything else.

They dived.

The lagoon was changing color again, bluer here.

Beyond the sunken church, and the hill that supported the tiny fisher island, was an avenue of pillars. On each was mounted a marble statue. They were of gods and heroes, classical, with faces melted by a century or more of the lagoon.

He passed them marveling, looking in their hyacinthine sightless eyes that seemed to follow him. He sensed their heads turning on white limestone necks. Could not catch them at it.

Fish small as fingernails, bright as mirrors, flushed between. He swam seventy feet above the place where the street had been, when men walked there.

He wanted to sink further, root through the palaces, among the waterlogged gardens where flamy anemones grew and caught their light, sift through his fingers the capitas of vanished emperors, the bronze pennies slung overboard for luck.

But the air was stale again, and he kept on after his guides.

Another shape came in his way. On a pedestal sat Neptune, turned to verdigris. Furian punched the trident and it broke off, spiraling down to the paving of the swallowed street below.

Nothing else was important. The world did not exist. You need not think.

He saw a transparent mermaid behind a wall. An hallucination probably, the dying air, or not.

And then the plan of streets and masonry gave way, and there unrolled beneath him an incredible vista of the ancient earth—an amphitheater of the Romans, many hundreds of feet across and more in length, an oval, whose tiers of seats cascaded to a dubious hollow floor. What cheering and screaming, what scenes of battle and death had been there, where now the milky water curled, and fishes eddied in their own cool and indifferent crowds. To go down to this was almost an imperative, to press on the stone and penetrate the walks beneath.

But just past this place was a wavering forest of the weed, and into it the divers were just now flickering.

Years on, would he recall this sight, and how he had been cheated of it? Maybe not. For there were other memories above.

He followed into the weed. As he did so, he saw the tendrils were strung by diamonds, emeralds, purple jacinth. Next moment the jewelry fled. Fish. After all, how like the bloody world.

A black tunnel roared. The divers proceeded into it.

Why go on? Why go on and come to land. Why trouble.

But instinct was too vigorous. He propelled himself also into the tunnel.

After a moment they were rising up again. Something sucked at them, some current from above.

They emerged into a chamber of blackest water, and the boy swam straight up and pushed at a huge lid in the roof. The lid unfolded, unhinging like a clam shell.

There was somber and unwelcoming light. Furian shot into it and his head was above the water.

The boy helped him out on to a shelf of wet stone, and undid the brace again from about his neck. Furian pulled off the globe and breathed a stinking clammy atmosphere far worse than staleness.

"Where is this?"

"The tomb vault of the ancient Ducemae of Venus," chanted the boy, crossing himself. "They're buried in lead boxes under the water."

Furian thought of the lead weight. He glanced about below, and saw through the water now, or thought he did, black coffin shadows, each surmounted by a prone granite figure.

"The Island of San Fumo."

"Yes, Signore."

The two others bobbed easily under the opened lid. They watched him, impartial yet unfriendly.

"I'd pay you," he said, "but alas. I think I may have been robbed in your house."

"You would have been, if you'd had anything."

"And you'd have earned every ducca."

The boy took Furian's globe, securing it to his belt. None of them was out of breath.

"The door to the vault is simple to force," said the man who talked. "It's already ajar."

The other did speak. He said, "All the men you know from the Mask Guild came to the Island. But their guild chapel is a mile or two away to the east from here. And they think you're dead, wouldn't you say."

"Yes, it's nicely convenient."

"But then," said the boy, "there is your lady."

"Which lady's that?"

"The butterfly lady."

"Oh, yes."

Furian shivered. It was dungeon-chill in the vault, and the water seemed finally warm. It was better here than the canals, and he had swallowed none of it. (And that was as well, because no one here would fold him in her arms, tend him, bring him back to health.)

The best course would be to go around the island, find some wanderer or fisher, get out to sea, to the larger shipping.

As for—as for the butterfly lady—she had shown her concern for him this time. Sitting at peace in the funeral boat as they flung him over.

"It's a shame," said Furian, "love doesn't last."

The boy said, "My sister told me, the lady wouldn't cry, though her father was dead."

Furian stood up. He said, "If I prayed any more, I'd speak for all of you."

"There are too many gods," said the talkative man.

He drew breath in one long, rushing, inward sigh, and sank straight down. The other did the same. The boy lingered,

"What is it? Do you want my coat?"

"Keep it, Signore. Try to light a fire and dry it. The night will be cold."

"You're too conscientious."

The boy spoke softly. "My sister said, your lady walked up and down, up and down. When a priest came, she sent him away. She wrote something, but then a masker went in and she hid it."

"She isn't my lady."

"Then she has no one now."

The boy drew in breath, leapt, turned in the air like a dolphin, and clove the water. He disappeared at once.

They had left Furian to replace the lid of the hidden entry. He did so, then climbed the passage from the stone shelf. Above was a ruinous chapel, full of loose stones and ivy. The iron door, as promised, cranked ajar, and needed only a shove or two to let him forth. He wrenched it back where it had been once he was out, and turned to see what the world now offered.

He was in a walled grove of elderly unflowering myrtle trees. On the gate was an old escutcheon of Venus, the star and goddess symbol, and the coronet of a Ducem. But the gates too were half open.

Beyond he saw the sweep of a hill, drenched in night, the cypresses standing like black pens, and the fields of little humps and markers and tiny statues, and here and there the great ghostly summerhouse of a mausoleum, fluttered by the merciless wings of basalt angels.

Over the slope, about two miles off, the sky was terra-cotta red, and the malevolent smoke funneled into heaven all the way to God.

The night smelled of ashes, and of dew. Of roses also. Of the most bitter and unacceptable flavors. But it was cold. And the boy had been right. A line of woods ran away to the left. He must make for those, (shoeless, maskless), and set to work the tinder he had somehow had and they had let him keep. Light a fire. Dry himself. Think of where next to take himself. Since it would not be back to her, then where?

# 3

THE ISLE OF DEATH WAS ALL in this fashion, the endless grave yards with their miniature graves, the occasional tall and imposing tomb. Through everything, the woods and orchards of the Island threaded, old trees girdled by late flowers, a statuesque oak, a beech, a pool of water with some funereal nymph, a willow leaning in sallowing autumn hair.

By night, everything was grisaille, or black or coal blue, or lit by the hell fires russet and priestly magenta.

He made his own fire soon, under the trees. He stripped when it was alight, and rubbed himself with clumps of the sandy grass. He dried his clothes, put them on again. He longed for brandy, more than any lost love. Or less? If she had been with him, would he have cared only for her? He would have held her, lain over her to keep warm. Sex for food and drink, and her sweetness to hold in faith.

Let her go. She was a bitch. She was insane and all the filthy things he had ever thought. She had let him be sent into the water. One shudder, one outstretched arm, however powerless. But not. Not she.

Her hands, so white. Her stroking, her caressing, her teasing of his body. Her full warm breasts, her slenderness, the wonder of the core of her. Her face. Which he had thought he had begun to read like his Bible.

Let her burn in hell. Let her *go*.


SOMETHING WAS MOVING in the wood. There had been bear and lynxes once on the Island, but no longer. (Although now and then, they or their revenants were sighted.) Probably rats, a large bird—But they did not wear boots.

Furian got up. He stood aside into the shadow of the trees, leaving the fire to burn. He had made a makeshift weapon, a stick sharpened in the flames. He toted it, ready.

Into the clearing came a man. His head was shaven, shining like tarnished copper in the firelight. On his shoulder was a magpie, also color-changed, black and pink from the glow.

Shaachen walked straight to the fire. He posed beside it, capering a little. "A friend and he hides." His little old female face stretched in an evil grin. "Come out, handsome." And the bird cawed.

Furian walked into the light.

"If you're here, I hope you'll be useful."

"What am I? Your saint? Of course I shall be useful. See what the old bugger has brought you."

Shaachen unslung his satchel. Out came a loaf and some cheese, a brandy bottle and a bloated skin of wine.

"Thank God," said Furian. He let himself down on the ground, and took the brandy, drinking off five or six raw gulps. "Last time you were no use, under the window acting beggars."

"My darling brought you up a letter."

"That was so much what I needed."

"The paper was invisibly traced with symbols of magic to keep you safe. It seems it has. Where is it now?"

"In my coat. It got wet." Furian felt for the letter and found a dryish mush.

"Keep it still," said the Doctor.

"And how did you find me this time?" said Furian. "And why did you bother?"

"I enjoy you," said Shaachen. "You are so flamboyantly much what I anticipate. It's like the play."

"My thanks."

"Don't mention it. As to finding you, I knew they would come here. I waited, watched. I saw the charon off and came after in a little fisher boat. At the Island all of them come forth—but for my dear Furian. So, you have escaped them."

"Didn't you see something drop in the water?"

"The charon was some way off. But yes, perhaps. Was that you?"

"It was me."

"You jumped and swam."

"They threw me in with lead on my feet."

Shaachen had sat down. He fed cheese slowly to the magpie. He said nothing; then, "But why would they do that?"

"Unlike yourself, they don't care for me."

"They hate you, doubtless. But I'd thought—perhaps not already having slain you—they must want to keep you. Didn't they offer to make you one of their own?"

"Yes. And how did you know *that*?"

"I too have been searching out, asking here and there. The guilds are known, in some form, to each other. I am an alchemist. Within my own circle, I may hear things not broadcast on the street. I might have

warned you, but you went too fast. Straight in at her
door, the Virgo with blue eyes. There was a rumor too,
of her. Is it true, her face doesn't move? Fachia Pietra. A
fascination."

"Her face. Her heart."

"Another rejection?

"She was willing enough. But when they drowned
me, she sat by serene as Sunday morning in the Primo."

"I begin to see," said Shaachen. "I begin to. Not quite."

"They kill for hire," said Furian. "Those who wear
the most celebrated masks seem to be their victims."

"Yes, I have that already. They are of few numbers.
Three or four men, forming a secret guild within the
Guild. Not all the rest are so tainted. This limits their
scope a little. You may trust me on this. But they kill for
hire, you say?"

"And to gratify some foul urge for chaos, power,
viciousness. God knows."

"And he—the raging one who showed his animal in
our rite?"

"What rite?" said Furian. He took some bread and
ate it. But he was hungry, and put it by...there was no
longer any reason to behave logically with drink or sleep
or food.

"You forget it so soon. When the Zodians towered in
my chamber, and I told you the murderers were in the
Mask Guild."

"Oh, that time. Yes. I remember the animal with a
barb on its penis. That was him, was it? Lepidus? Well,
he was angry with her. With me. With everyone who had
something he hadn't, or cheated him in some way, as he
saw it. He must be a bellowing ghost. He's dead."

"Ah!" Shaachen exclaimed. "I see more. How do
you know he died?"

"I saw his corpse and so did she. Its whole face was off. He was our ally, or presently he was. Someone didn't find pleasure in that, and had him seen to, and I was next. But she knew. Either that, or she didn't mind it." Furian stood up. He said loudly, too loudly for the wood, "She sat and watched them throw me over. She couldn't speak, but in extremity she could make a sound—I know, I heard it over and over in her bed. She didn't even rise, or *fidget*."

"But they had hold of you," said Shaachen. "two or three of them, surely, to be certain. And there were the other men on the charon. What could she do?"

"Nothing, nothing. But in God's name—not one flick of her hand."

"Sit," said Shaachen. "Tell me how you came here with lead feet. I've been searching you out for a great while."

Furian sat. He took the wine skin and drank. He told Shaachen of the divers and the underwater entry at the tomb of ancient Ducemae. All the glamour of the journey was gone now. He knew Shaachen would have been avid for descriptions of the drowned City, the statues, the amphitheater, and withheld them meanly. Furian was tired with the old tiredness which precluded sleep.

Shaachen did not inquire anything about the swim, the tomb, apparently aware of this. The magpie drowsed on Shaachen's shoulder. It was young and splendid as a new-minted coin, and knew the tricks of the dead. The loyalty too. Some were loyal. Could you only expect it from a beast or a bird?

"Did you keep the fishing boat by the Isle?" Furian asked. "We can use it to go back. Then I have a choice, it seems to me. To make inland from the City, or take ship elsewhere. I might evade them now they think they've done for me."

"This is your sole choice?" said Shaachen.

"I think so. They revel in what they do, but I'm a small enough fish to them."

"But no," said Shaachen, "I think not."

Furian blasphemed softly and obscenely. "I've had sufficient of this, Dianus Shaachen. I'm off to save my worthless life."

"And hers? Is that also worthless?"

"To me, yes, if she thinks nothing of mine."

Shaachen took the magpie from his shoulder. He held it in both hands and cooed to it and kissed its demonic head. The beak, which could have taken out his eyes, stayed still as carving. It made back to him a silly little love-cackle.

"Consider," said Shaachen, "unlike other women, she can't speak to plead for you, or beg you to await her in heaven. And surrounded by the men who are enemies, she is without physical recourse. Consider, perhaps, she's as shocked as yourself to see you suddenly bound and thrown to your death. All of her turns in terror to stone. You pierced her body, but did you possess her brain? How do you know she betrays you, or has no concern. Perhaps, as you sank, she fell dead on the deck from the agony of what had happened."

"You saw them leave their boat. Was she dead, then?"

Shaachen said, with grizzly lugubriousness, "She walked heavily, like a woman sick or half asleep."

"She was a little tired. Bored by such an uneventful day."

"No, Furian Furiano. She walked as if she were laden down. With lead."

Furian slung the wine away.

"She has no friends with them, that's all. Dreads them. She had a friend in me and didn't want me, any more then she wanted del Nero that she let them kill two feet from her sublime blue sala. Or in front of her, even, as she thought I'd been."

"Only suppose," said Shaachen, "there is one chance you may be wrong. That she loves you and her heart, which isn't stone like her face, but glass, like the hearts of all lovers, is in little bits, cutting her breast. Only suppose she's in the Mask Guild's grip and thinks you dead, and can't cry her tears of alabaster. And you sit here to speak of foreign ships."

"In Christ's bleeding name—"

Shaachen let the magpie loose. It flew round the clearing, with claps of its ink and paper feathers, gleaming with fire, sheened red now, not blue.


As they walked the night Island, Furian swore at the ground, bombarding his shoeless feet. Shaachen muttered. Finally, "Give me back the paper I sent you."

"That letter is porridge."

"Scrape it out. I want it."

Furian did as Shaachen said, scooping up the glutinous, crumbling mess from a pocket. Shaachen took it and stowed it in his coat.

"You think I won't need your magic symbols of protection any more? Why didn't you bring boots?"

"You'll need only Doctor Shaachen."

"Oh well. I can't argue with that."

The hills coursed up, whorled with the tiny, circling graves. They passed a monument to some great family of Venus. The goddess herself mourned them in marble.

Pines and cypress pointed at the black sky, where stars were hung out like sparkling masks. (Too far off to see their eyes.) A nightingale sang.

Furian thought, *I said I'd go to her, because of what he said to me. Why is he here? He experiments on the dead and on the living. One more experiment?*

The wine-bloom of the burning chimneys had lessened. They went east towards the Mask Guild chapel.

It was, in any event, a lost cause. And probably she was as base as he had thought. But if not, if not—

DAWN TURNED THE SMOKES of San Fumo violet. Birds spurted their music, and it was possible to sense the lagoon's lapping, as if only darkness had muffled it.

There were groves of trees, and then an open slope, the autumn grass turned to the sun, tobacco brown. Above, a walled garden with acacia and cypresses. From these, a golden dome rose like a sun's egg.

"The Mask Chapel," said Shaachen, complacently. "How do you mean to proceed?"

"Limping. Look about. Do you know anything?"

"The chapel will be difficult of access. Your best means are to go knock on the door."

"You think so?"

"It will save you time."

Furian said, "My one advantage was, I thought, they believed me dead."

"Don't be too sure," said Shaachen. "Maybe not."

They went up the slope, carelessly. There was little cover, some small groups of parched trees turned towards the lagoon, which now they saw far off. The water was blue and the City lay over it, a transparent vertical map of towers, floating, as ever, like a flock of ships.

Beyond the dome of the chapel, one smoke rose.

Shaachen spoke unintelligibly to the magpie. It lifted straight up, and flew back among the trees.

There was no gate in the wall. An arch showed a flat path, set with mosaic chariots racing—they were chariots of Death with sable horses. The building at the path's end was simple but ornate, a windowless box. But there were windows sliced narrowly in the dome. Behind, buildings clustered in the garden.

A woman was coming down the path, unexpected and incongruous. She wore a festive blood-red dress, and her face was hidden by a black fan mask.

She hurried, and as she came closer, Shaachen stood away behind Furian. Furian glanced at him and saw the Doctor had put on a comic mask, a rabbit with tall ears.

"What are you playing at?"

"I'm now your servant, a poor old fool. Call me Diano."

Calypso reached them. She put out her hand and lightly prodded at Furian's breast.

"Is it you?"

"Who?" he said.

"You must come in quickly. I don't like it outside."

She took his arm, and snuggled against him. As she pulled on him, they began to walk, and rabbity Shaachen crept behind.

The black and gilded door of the chapel had opened and Lunario Moon-Mask was there, with a couple of men behind him. These men carried staves, but Lunario's hands were empty.

"What a long while you were," he said.

Calypso made a scratching movement at her mask, as if it itched. She kept hold of Furian.

"I made haste," she said. "There—are creatures in the garden. Was that why you sent me?"

"Hush. I refer to our guest, who dallied."

Furian said, as they came to the door, "I had to return from the dead."

Lunario laughed. "But I know that's a lie, Signore Furian."

Furian eased Calypso off his arm. She turned abruptly and slapped his face a hard, stinging blow, then stalked into the chapel, past the grinning half-masked men.

Lunario said, "She's got a strong arm. Did you feel the slap? Does it prove to you you're alive?"

"I supposed I was meant to be drowned."

"Not at all. The divers rescued you as they were paid to do. You came ashore at the old tomb. Then you might have run away, or run here, but you delayed. Now you've arrived at last. Who's this one?" Lunario gestured at Shaachen, who was hopping and twittering at Furian's back.

"A servant. Somehow he followed me. Senile, as you see."

"Senile but clever. Well, he can come in." Lunario stood aside. The men with staves stood aside. How welcoming.

Beyond them, a black stone vestibule gave on a second massive door, shut fast.

Lunario turned and moved into a narrow passage. Calypso went after him, ignoring Furian now, and the men with staves gave him one friendly urging. He followed, and Shaachen, gibbering, perhaps dribbling in an excess of theatricality, scuttled at his back.

They ascended steps. A lamp burned dully on the wall.

"Wait here. Your servant may wait, too."

Lunario crossed the space they had entered, and was gone into another corridor. Only one of the men with staves remained. But Calypso slunk against Furian. "I see things. They're there. Only I can see them. There's something black clinging to you. It has claws, but no face."

"Go after you master," Furian said.

Calypso bridled. "This mask," she said, "sees better than I do." In the eyeplaces, her own eyes darted, inflamed and congested, seeming half blind.

Furian sat on a stone bench by the wall. He smiled down at the floor. In a few more moments she scudded away, her bloody skirts sweeping up the old rank dusts off the paving.

Diano, the insane servant, crouched on the floor. He had taken out some dice and was throwing them, grunting and giggling at the results.

"I'd have them put down," said the man with the stave. "Once they get like that."

"You're right," said Furian.

"You wouldn't keep a dog like it."

"No."

"How did he manage to follow you?"

"He comes over to the graves sometimes. He has relatives buried here. It was just bad luck we met."

The man with the stave approached and bent over Shaachen. "Eh, rabbit. I'd wring your scrawny neck." Shaachen Diano looked up at him. The rabbit mask leered. "And he's a Jew. Shit-scum. I'd burn the lot."

Furian got up. He had nothing to lose, it was mostly all gone. He hit the man with considerable force, and in a shower of gore and broken teeth he went over and lay there. Furian picked up the stave, and at that moment another man came in from the corridor. This one laughed luxuriantly. "I can't leave you alone for one moment, can I? Didn't the wetting cool you down?"

"Evidently not."

Furian observed this newcomer. A stocky man, with the mask of a wolf. Its maned fur passed over his head and down his broad back, concealing hair and throat. The voice nagged, for it was known—and the mask known too. It came in a flash of seconds. The reveler in the Groves of Diana, who had seized Messalina off the altar, nearly nude, and galloped her away into the wild park.

"You're here, I think, for her," he said now, the wolf, in his rich, *known* voice.

"Who's that?"

"Your girl with blue eyes."

"But I was meant to be here," said Furian.

"If you cared a lot for her, you'd come after her. Simple enough. And you haven't disappointed."

"Or drowned."

"You were previously warned, Furian, an ordeal lay before you, your initiation into the Guild. So far, you've come through the testing well."

Furian took a breath. "The drowning was—an initiation?"

"A part of it. There's more. For now, you should take rest. There are things you must be told."

"Which I shan't credit."

"I think you may."

He made a short, dismissive motion. On his hand a black ring blazed like a living eye. It was the ring of Lepidus. He had, too, the wolf, the voice of Lepidus.

Furian said nothing.

The wolf said to him, "Come with me now. No

tricks or snares. My daughter's waiting for you in a little room."

As they walked, crazy Diano rattling in their wake, Furian said bleakly, "Who was the man you killed, the man whose face you cut away?"

"A custom of the Orichalci," said the wolf.

"I know. You told me once."

"I didn't think you listened."

Furian was trembling at a numb and somber distance from himself. Had *she* known it too, all along? That her father lived, that Furian would be saved. The lagoon was only a *test*, the sorcerous alchemical element of water.

"But the man," he said.

"Someone who resembled me bodily, somewhat," said Lepidus the wolf. "A ruffian, of no great use. We gave him a good dinner and drugged his wine. He was peacefully dead before I took off his face."

"Oh, then, it was inoffensive. As with Juseppi, too, I trust. A good dinner and some wine, before the torture and the Death of Osiris, the cutting in ten or eleven segments,

"Eleven, of course. It served only one most urgent purpose, to terrify, to close up doors and seal them. But it was done ritualistically because, for us, ritual has importance."

"And the faceless man I took for you, why that? Why not you aboard the boat, and throw me in yourself?"

"To come at you, Furian. To play upon you."

"Consider me come at and played on."

"I see you underestimate yourself. The hub of alchemy is the changing of lead into gold. But first the lead, which is so dark and set and strong, must be softened."

There was a door.

Behind it, apparently, she was. But was he ready for her?

The wolf put a key into the lock. And that might be one more illusion, a pretense that she was her father's prisoner here.

"There's so much to tell you, Furian. You'll marvel at it."

"I'm already overwhelmed."

"And now, the love of your heart."

The door folded wide.

It was a little side room of prayer, with an icon of Beautiful Maria.

She—Eurydiche—sat in a wooden chair. She wore still the black gown from the charon, and the opals dressed her hair. Her face was unmasked, but turned away. Perhaps she had turned it even as the door opened, as a normal woman might, to hide what, in her, was always anyway quite hidden.

She appeared untouched. Like the icon on the wall.

"Now, Doctor Shaachen," said Lepidus mildly, "let's leave these lovers to their reunion. There's much to do, and I can allow the eager young man only one hour in her company. But it should be private."

Mad Diano babbled.

Lepidus said, "Or, if you prefer to be senile, Doctor, I can put you into a sewage pit we have here, for just such emergencies."

Shaachen straightened. He said, "Why join the Mask Guild and not my own, the Guild of Alchemists?"

"I was too modest, Doctor, to essay your guild."

"But you're easily wise enough," said Shaachen. "Some join us who can do nothing. And you can do so much."

"I shall have to see to your death," said Lepidus.

"All men come to death," said Shaachen, "I've been shown, it's nothing. Only let me see the ritual through. The *spell*. I'd like to witness your skill to its full."

"Since you ask so nicely, perhaps. Meanwhile, someone must take away your satchel."

The door shut and the key turned in the lock. Shaachen and his death, Lepidus and his life, were gone.

There was only the small room, and Eurydiche sitting there, her face turned away.

Furian looked levelly around and into every corner. It was an instinct. There was no method for her to write. Someone had been very sure of that. Or else she had not asked. For what could she say to him?

Shaachen, the idiot, had sold himself to a murderer for nothing. And it was Shaachen who had persuaded Furian to this spot. The word of an idiot was worth what his death had cost—nothing.

Yes, there had been *one chance* she was innocent and in despair. But she had known it all, and been accomplice to it all. This now, was simply to be more softening of the lead.

He walked to her chair and stood looking down at her. "I'll ask you my questions, and you must nod or shake your head. If you won't, then so be it. Of course, what you indicate will doubtless be a lie. But even so, I want it from you. I want to see you tell me the truth or the falsehood. Because you are the reason for all my woes, and for all the woes of all this story, aren't you, my little stone doll?"

# 4

Eurydiche raised her head. She rose, and he drew back. Only the edge of her dress brushed over his hand, and at the touch of it, he shivered.

She made no other gesture. Her arms hung at her sides. Eyes. Face. Doll indeed.

"Very well," he said, "Yes or No, then. When he lay on the floor of your room, I mean the man they killed and defaced, did you know this wasn't Lepidus, your father?"

Her head moved instantly, side to side. No.

So, it was a game she wanted.

Furian said, "Thank you, Madama, for your first delightful lie." But she did not move. He had already explained he would not believe denials. Perhaps this enhanced her clandestine amusement. (Had she always laughed at him? Even flat on her back? But no—her physical heart and her loins could not lie. There at least she had told the truth. A slut who would take pleasure from any able man.) "Tell me then, when they threw me over, did you know I was to live?" Her head, side to side. Obviously, deliriously, No. He said, smiling, "Why then, if you didn't know, did you show no sign of alarm? Let me suggest—you'd lost consciousness from shock and pain." But her head went side to side. He said, "You were quite helpless and didn't dare to move? Overcome by your enormous grief, you sat mourning the two deaths—his and mine."

At this, her hands did come up. It was a strange almost involuntary movement, as if she wished to grasp at something. But nothing was there. Her hands fell. She nodded very slowly. Yes.

"Poor girl," he said. "And not even able to weep at your hurt. Losing me, your great love."

A tumult rose in him and he gripped his brain and blood and held them down. He wanted to strike her face as he had struck the sneering globule of the Jew-hater. He wished to smash the porcelain of her. And he clenched his hands upon his arms as if he froze, to keep from killing her.

"What a bitch you are," he said. "You've known it all. That he slaughters for hire, and for his fun. Now a rich patron cretinous enough to order a mask from his artisans, and now a fellow off the street, solely in order to upset little Furian the dupe. And you, you were at the Revels of Diana, to watch as he prepared some filthy plan for that woman there, poor bloody Messalina. In some way he works through you—How? What does he do? But you can't tell me without your pen and paper, and anyway, I doubt you would."

She shied from him all at once. She sank back in the chair, and put one arm over its wooden side, and put her head down on her arm.

"I've distressed you. I'm so sorry. We were such friends, weren't we. And I came back here for you. Or could I even have escaped? Perhaps not. The plot's as thick as a stew, as the idiot said. Could I even trust the trees of the Island?"

In turn he put his back to her. He stood before the door, to wait out the hour.

As his breathing calmed, he heard her breathing, then. It was throaty, stifled.

Furian knew a moment's terror at what they had come down to. He could not harm her. Her beauty was more dear to him that his life. God knew why. The beauty of her inner self, the being that had looked out at him through blind-blue windows. The being he had held and loved.

He said, harshly, "Don't be frightened, Eurydiche. I won't assault you. You've been more cunning than I thought. I'm still in thrall to you. I'm yours. A worthless gift, I know."

Some while after, she came to him so softly he did not realize, lost in his thoughts of nothing, until he heard her gown on the floor.

She moved about him and took his hand. As once before, she let her head droop on his chest. He said, "Let's not, Eurydiche. It's enough I'm enslaved. I won't play your game any more. Go back and sit in the chair."

At this she left him. Her warmth, her perfume, and her self. He did not look.

In the furnace, the lead melted down. But Furian was not a substance to be changed to gold. He knew as much. He knew they would fail with him, and then he must die. He did not quite see how it was to be, but that it must be.

All his life among the dark had led him here. At eighteen, when he left his father's house, he had been on the road to this.

He could have ended a hundred ways. Of some knife. Of some sickness in the warrens of the City. Even, once or twice, of starvation. But no, fate brought him to the Isle of the Dead to die. Fate was a poetess.

\* \* \*

WHEN, SEEMINGLY, THE HOUR was up, the door was unlocked. The man masked as the bull loomed there, with two unknown others.

Furian went out, and the bull conducted him downstairs and out of the chapel building, across the guild burial garden whose markers showed large and pale between the acacias and the stiff sculpted yews.

Stoically, almost sleepily, Furian made no attempts at action or evasion. He was taken into another building with a lesser dome, this of lapid blue, and so to a chamber with hospitable appurtenances, a couch, a bath, even some books laid by.

The bull offered him a steady hand to shave his face. Furian laughed. Said No. The bull insisted. For business to come, he must be at his best.

"Oh, *yes*, then. Watch the razor doesn't slip. They want their meat unsliced."

Afterwards there was a meal, with wine, and fruit.

Would it be achievable, the state of sleep? How could it be. That phase was over. And soon, a longer sleep. (The same for Shaachen, who thought it would be otherwise.)

Yet Furian dreamed for five minutes in a chair, and saw Lepidus' substitute skull, symbol of all death.

Fresh linen had been left out, and a new set of noble clothes. He did not bother with them. If they wanted his refinement, they would have to insist.

The body anyway was the suit of clothes, and under the body were the indecent bones. And under those, a soul, perhaps, or not a soul.

The day gathered and spun towards an evening, long skeins of light that put gold-leaf on to the high unseeing slot in the wall. Once a bird passed by. Was it Shaachen's magpie? A symbol opposed to the Skull, one of everlasting existence and renewal. The Virgin's bird also, Virgo . . .

He thought of insubstantial, anguished things. His mother's outcry when he had gone away. Cupid in her rose-yellow bed complaining that he had given her up and heaping invective on him. Men he had cut open. The child crying outside the tavern because two bastards abused her with words, too young to answer or know how to run away.

Sunfall, dusk, these went on and on. A man before his execution, Furian felt obliged to look at them, take note. How saffron gave way to madder, and so to mallow.

But he was impatient with life now, parading herself. Another beauty trying to deceive, when reasonless night was so obviously close.

# 5

MIDNIGHT HAD JUST STRUCK, when they came.

They told him this.

But he was waiting.

No comment was made on his unchanged garments, stained from the lagoon and the smoke of a fire. He had put on the shoes only. There had been no mask.

They went back the way they had come, and so out into the garden.

The sky was blackest blue and the moon had risen, waning and fragile, a slender, graceful girl. Moonlight spotted the tombs, leopardine shadows. They reached a wall of the chapel. There was a door, and this they undid for him. He was to go through.

Lepidus was in the room, standing, a genial host. One recalled his faultless manners as an agent and traveler. His wit and finesse, and how he had never seemed put out, with all the resentment and contempt smoldering, invisible.

He too was unmasked. Perhaps he had extra entertainment in acting this out, his face schooled to such spurious and insulting, avuncular charm.

"Furian. Take a seat, and try this wine." Furian took the seat, and the wine. He drank a mouthful and put it

by. "So abstemious all at once? Well, that's to your credit. You may want to be able to think."

"Yes I may."

"I have to tell you of certain events. Before we come
to guild matters."

Furian said, "What's next? Fire, earth or air?"

"Nothing so straightforward. Consider the lagoon,
if you will, as fluidity rather than the element of water.
The mutable and transient—Neptune. There's only one
more trial of you. You may not even mind it. May like it.
We'll see."

Furian said nothing.

Lepidus sat down in the chair opposite, and poured
himself a glass of the wine. The chamber was not large,
but hung with sober velvet. Another door led somewhere. The lion's den?

Lepidus spoke low, in an encompassing and com-
panionable way, (Furian was put in mind of some priest
benighted with him at an inn.)

"Almost, Furian, I stand as a father to you now."

"A father. But I left my father."

"So you did. And why was that?"

"A complex and irksome tale, Lepidus. I don't have
your flare for story-telling. I won't weary you."

"Then I shall tell you, Furian, shall I, your own
story?"

Furian said nothing. But now he waited.

Lepidus said, "Once or twice, I saw you as a boy.
You were impressive for your years. I remember, you
had a special talent for music—"

"You embarrass me."

"But also you were very impertinent to me."

"Was I. I don't recall."

"Of course not. They were little things."

"I didn't always stay to listen," said Furian.

"That night," said Lepidus, "that night you were eighteen and newly home, you spent your time gawking at a young woman's breasts across the table."

Furian laughed shortly. "I do remember that."

"Well, you were immature, and had been studious. I was wrong in what I did."

Furian said, too swiftly, "And what did you do?"

"I've got your interest now. I'm glad. I did a foolish thing, almost what a woman might have done, if able. I put a little spell on you."

Furian's throat closed hard. He tried to swallow, and could not. He sucked air into his lungs and said, off-handedly "To make me love you instead?"

"I might not have minded it, Furian Furiano. A taste of you in your youth. There are more pleasures that way than one. But no, it wasn't for love."

Furian waited again. He did not dare to speak, and in his breast his heart was clammering, in tight iron strokes. Had he always partly guessed? *Something*—

"When I was among the Orichalci and the Argenti of the Amarias," said Lepidus, leaning back, the raconteur again, "I learnt some of their formulae, their arts. To get anywhere with them, a man had to take on some of their nature, and go through particular endurances. It was worth while, although I carry scars, both physical and of the psyche, to this day. A treacherous and wondrous people, that tribe, The Enemy. It was only a little, little spell. The sort they'd use to turn a man away from their hunting grounds, or from a woman. Or from his kindred."

Lepidus paused, and Furian heard the silence of the close, draped room, loud as a whistling gushing wave from the sea.

"And to turn me from what, exactly."

"Your then life. Its happiness and content. To make you dissatisfied. Disturbed. Want other things. Oh, maybe I had some notion you might seek me out for adventure. I would have liked it, Furian, to show you the world as I'd discovered the world to be. But it was a fact, your passion was too strong for me. It took my tiny hex and turned it to a massive stroke. You left everything and ran into the dark."

Furian looked away. He looked into the insubstantial, wavering past. To his father's estate, the stairway in the folding up of the candles. A score of pale wings fluttering down, and there, *between one step and the next*. So swift.

(He had been puzzled. Trying to work it out. It was elusive and ran before him, lashing its tail. Yet it had led him on.) Disillusionment. Guilt. Emptiness. That dawn at the window and the soft wind blowing up the Veneran plain. The days of lotuses over.

But it was not possible that Lepidus had been so accomplished. To drive him out of his mind, to exile him from his family, to diminish him among the slums and sinks of Venus—*to make him into what he was*—

He said, very dry, "I'm to believe all that was your doing, then. How you amaze me, Lepidus. And I thought you only a showy vagabond."

Lepidus bowed. "You're at liberty, of course, to disbelieve. But I've had you in my fist since that night. When I watched you, when I forgot you, you were mine. I created you, Furian. Even your actorish name."

Furian took up the wine. He had a pair of mouthfuls. Lepidus observed, amused, it seemed, or so he pretended.

The simplest means to get a man into your power

was to inform him he was there already.

And Lepidus began to talk again, as if he enjoyed this so much, he could not hold back.

"Even with her, with my daughter, I like to think it was some element of my labor on you that drew you precisely to her. Even to finding del Nero's mask on the canal that *fateful* morning. A dog follows its master, even when he doesn't call."

"I'm not your dog."

"Are you your own then? Eh? Would you say so?"

Furian took another mouthful of the wine. He had finished it after all, and his tormentor saw, and came at once, so solicitous, to refill the cup.

Furian said, "That was a quaint story. Now tell me one about Shaachen."

"The Doctor? Oh, he must die. I think he knows not only what our inner guild does, but perhaps just how we do it."

Lightly Furian said, "Can't I buy you off with something? He's an old dunce. Nearly what he was acting for you with his rabbit mask."

"I don't think you mean what you say. A fool, yes; or why else come here after you. But a learned fool. Among his books and potions I wouldn't trust him. But he carries little in his head, save curious illusions for drunk princes."

"Let him live. You promised me my life. Or is that changed?"

"No. I'm like any kind father. You're to be my heir. You'll have my daughter, and a function within the guild."

"But I don't want your daughter."

Lepidus beamed upon him. "You must understand, I have servants in her house who are useful to me. Do you remember the girl who threw a shoe at your head?"

Furian got up. He stood by the chair. He said, "So it was all spied on."

"What else? Your idyll sounds most enchanting. You were made for each other, it seems . . . both by me. The musician loved her but she was only generous to him. You've no notion how apt this will be. The hatred you feel for her, the love, the distaste, the distrust—the fury."

"Like your own? Or don't I measure up to you?"

Lepidus now laughed very loudly. He looked hugely tickled, gratified.

"Can it be you deduced so much?"

Furian hesitated. "What do you mean now?"

"Let me tell you then. I've had her. She was fifteen.'

Furian felt a panic-stricken cacophony rising in him, black as the pits of hell, and with their heat. He pushed it away and said, but his voice sounded cracked and old, "You fucked your daughter."

"Divinely, three or four times. I was so disgusted by her, but she was so dewy, soft, so arousing. What else?"

In the depths of his mind, Furian saw the animal of rage with the barb upon its phallus, rearing amid trampled sparks.

"You want to ask me, did she like it. How can I know? She didn't resist. Or encourage. And naturally she neither wept nor frowned nor screamed out in pain or ecstasy. In her writings to me after, she never once referred to it."

Furian picked up the wine. Then he let the glass fall, shattering on the floor.

He said, "You made her your whore, and then the whore of others, to come at them. Del Nero and who else? You meanwhile lay over the others who were women, such as Messalina."

"And a man or two . . . but otherwise you have it. Yes, Furian. Sex is a component of what I did to them. You see, these weren't like the little spell I set on you. These are the arts of murder."

Eurydiche, whore and accomplice. Maybe the willing mistress of her father. Eurydiche—disgust, arousal.

Furian stood behind the chair.

Lepidus sat drinking at his ease. He looked well-fed. As if he had just been dining.

A huge wind of fire seemed to have rushed through the room. But it was gone.

A knock sounded gently on the inner door.

Lepidus put aside his glass.

"Let's go down now and complete the ritual."

"Yes, let's, since I haven't a choice."

"The technique of it I'll explain to you, at the proper moment. But you're primed."

Furian turned to him. He said, with no control, hoarsely, wildly, like a boy of eighteen, "Don't trust me, Lepidus. Don't ever do that. I'll be obedient. I'll keep my place. One day or night I'll settle with you."

"I'll look forward to it. You and I and a little tussling. How appetizing."


OUTSIDE THE DOOR, A WALL, and one more corridor that ran in two directions. Lepidus went away to the left, and Furian was led decorously to the right by the bull-masked man.

Furian was compliant. Without argument or struggle. For what was it to be now—some rank magic, some vicious, scar-making infliction learnt from the tribe called The Enemy—what significance did it have? He had revealed his namesake fury, fury and shame, his weakness, all of it. He had retained nothing that could be handy. Even if Lepidus had lied about his 'little spell', (he had lied, he *must* have lied), he had made Furian his creature.


THE INNER HALL OF THE chapel was of some size and perfectly round. Above, it rose into the arena of the dome, which here was faced with black marble, like all the chamber. Eyelets had been cut in the fabric of the dome, but they were small, and revealed only further darkness, the black marble ceiling of the night.

Below, the floor was glassy, like polished obsidian. Shallow black steps rose from it, and around the walls at the top of this terrace, were placed a ring of braziers that leapt with bloody flame. And the flames reflected upward into the roof, downward into the floor.

Within the black circle of the floor was marked, by narrow inlaid tiles, a white square. At the point of each angle, on the terrace above the steps, bulked a black marble chair with a high arched back.

Alchemically, conceivably, these points and chairs marked the Cardinals of the compass, North, South, West and East.

There was nothing else in the round hall but for the three human shapes left, as if stranded, on the lower floor.

Each poised alone, isolated, like a chess-piece on an emptied board.

Furian saw the woman Calypso, in her black fan mask, and scarlet dress. And perhaps twenty feet away from her, the woman Eurydiche. They had changed her clothes. Now she was clad almost like the Virgin, a white gown, and caught from a coronet in her hair, a blue smoke of veil. A diamond spangled on her forehead, the star of Venus. She was not masked. Yet, masked.

Shaachen, sitting near the center of the floor, had kept his rabbit's face. Also kept up or put back his invented character. He was idly tossing his dice on to the floor with an annoying, unbearable clinking, retrieving them, throwing them again. The satchel was gone, and anything it might have contained with it. He looked very small and black, a pathetic, pitiable form. Of all of them, he should not be here. But then, he had asked to witness the ritual. A show-off himself, he had unerringly sensed the same in Lepidus. But as Lepidus had guessed, removed from his props, powders, tinctures, chalk, book—Shaachen was powerless.

Furian did not go down the steps. He looked at the upper tier on to which he had come out. The door was no longer to be seen. Now his eyes grew accustomed to the braziers' jumping arson, he saw golden outlines traced on the inner dome. All the beasts and figments of the zodiac were there, and the constellations, gods in chariots, unicorns and dragons, which seemed to move—his head reeled. He turned his glance back to the floor.

He looked at her. But Eurydiche made no movement, if she noted him. Her body was still as a stem no wind could blow.

His eyes left her. And he beheld, with sudden surprise, almost affront, Calypso's bodice had been altered. Above the scarlet stuff, her oval, heavy breasts were sumptuously bare. She did not seem to notice. Keeping to where she had stood or been put to stand, she turned her fan-face here and there, up and down. She called to Furian in a fish-wife's screech: "Be careful of them! They sting."

He thought, *Her breasts perhaps. Yes, they'd sting.* He thought of filling his hands with them, playing the tips of his fingers over them until she clutched him. She liked men. It would not take long.

But these thoughts did not belong in this place. (What had been in Lepidus' hospitable wine?)

A fearful sound stamped in the hollow chamber. It was a drum. It beat once, then over and over. Its tempo was like a heart. The heart irresistibly picked up its rhythm.

Four figures were at the Cardinal points of the square, on the terrace at the top of the steps. They had come in through the walls at other now invisible entrances. In the dancing flame-light, such appearances were manageable.

Each figure was naked, and each was masked, the entire head covered over. Four heavy muscular men, (the fourth with curious, well-knit scars on the tawny material of his body.) They had each been shaved of every hair. One had the head of a shark, of silky slate grey. One the head of a white bear, whose fur ran down his neck. One had a face composed of a black vapor of bats with tiny winking eyes. The fourth one was a red wolf, its pelt pouring to his shoulders.

They walked about the chairs and sat in them. Four living statues with the heads of demon animals. And one, only one, the wolf, with his member swollen, ruddy and upright, which as he sat, he fingered, approvingly. A golden ring surrounded his erection, ornamenting and maintaining it. Lepidus. Lepidus in the station of the East, for the East was the wolf, the east wind howled with its voice. And the bats were the evening West, the shark the oceanic South. the white bear the cold and legendary North, the White Lands. Argenti masks, Orichalci.

From inside the head of the wolf, Lepidus spoke. His voice was almost a whisper, but the chamber carried it.

The words were Latin. Furian did not comprehend them. From Shaachen's mysteries he recognized the first swirling prickling of the air, and what might come, but did not care. Probably he could even understand the chant, for they had taught him Latin once. But he had made himself forget—

Whatever was wanted, he would have to do it. This was what he had confused with death—the death of the will. Until that day or night he had prophesied. Then he would rebel and Lepidus would kill him. Tonight anyway, he had lost all of himself.

And was she laughing? Would she like to have him after. The slave brought in chains to her bed. And again, the stab of desire, so he was erect as Lepidus, under his clothes.

The Guardians of the Guild chapel were rising. They were only partly visible, red and roiling, with fires for manes. The drum beat and the heart ran with the drum. A new chanting came, far, far off, across the continents perhaps. There were feathers in the flames and faces almost of men, painted black and cobalt and crimson. Winged men, and men with the lower bodies of stags. Things from the otherwhere. Sacred images of The Enemy.

Calypso was turning about on the floor. Maybe she thought she saw only what she had already been seeing. Some thing had taken hold of her mind; possibly she had truly seen these things before they were conjured.

But Eurydiche stood like stone. Familiar, all this, to her?

And Shaachen the alchemist sat in his rabbit mask,

the unmagical dice put away now. Very likely he was only intrigued. For the magpie had shown him he would live beyond death.

The Guardians merged into a laval fog. Behind each of the four chairs towered, for a moment the effigy of the mask, red wolf, great bear, a writhing shark, a flight of huge bats. Then they were gone.

Furian looked straight up again. In the dome, the zodiac and the stars and planets were wheeling slowly. The chariots jolted, the archer took aim, from the pitcher poured a torrent of fireworks. And Virgo was courted by the unicorn.

"Furian," said Lepidus intimately, in his ear.

But Lepidus sat on his seat of blackness some feet away, fondling himself with a deathly constraint.

"Furian, come here. I'll tell you the final secret, and what you must do."

On the floor, Shaachen turned his rabbit face to goggle at the wolf.

Furian, subject, went along the terrace to Lepidus.

"What's the secret? Do you want me to toss you off? My apologies."

Lepidus laughed. His laugh was honey.

"You can't break the sorcery, little boy, with little jibes. The energy is too strong. We four keep all the Guild at bay. We four will presently rule the Guild. All Venus, why not—worlds and powers."

"I'm here. Tell me the secret."

"Don't be impatient. Look at Calypso. Isn't she a splendid dish?"

"But you've sent her crazy, like Messalina."

"Not I, Furian. Not I. *It's the mask.*"

"I thought so. Like the others."

"Like the others. The prince who slew himself and

the lady who hanged herself. Del Nero who drowned himself and lies under the canal, looking up through the water. And Messalina, whose heart just stopped in the Madhouse. And so on. Always, the mask. Shall I say how?"

"By all means."

Furian's mouth was dry. The brazier heat was like hell for sure. And in the upper air, the golden elementals coiled about each other, and the furnaces of the Orichalci shifted with eyes and paint. Who wanted wine? Wine was red and hot. Water. Water from a stagnant pool. The poison of the canal, where he had swum to her, and del Nero's face had been turned up to him unseen, below.

"Listen," said Lepidus. "A mathematic. We learn intimately the facts of each victim. Their day and hour of birth, their totems and signs, their preferences and antipathies. Their deepest fears and joys. Their concealed perversities. Which planet rules them. How their inmost life is shaped. This is a minor exercise. Men love to talk of themselves, and where not, their underlings adore to betray them. There is magic too, a helpful knack. It's possible to discover, now and then, that which even the victim does not know of himself with his waking mind. When all *is* known, we make the mask. It's exquisite. It is the best of them, superficially. They must have it. They are complimented on all sides. But oh, the mask, where it touches them, on their skin, *there*. It has been made against everything they are. Against name and nature, condition and desire, heart and spirit. At the wrong phase of the moon, under the most unsuitable star. At an hour abhorrent to them, in the worst planetary conjunction our arts reveal. If they are up, we make *down*. If their tone is sweet we make *bitter*, and sweet for sour. A color they hate, present though never seen, a scent they loathe but will never smell—yet something of them smells and sees. Visualize a window set crooked in its frame. A wound that is unseen but never heals. It grinds, it grinds on them, and they never know how it is that it does. Evening for morning, day for night. And while it *grinds*, it stays a partner to what they are, inevitable, attached, like the shadow thrown on the wall. It binds them. Them must wear it, that mask, like no other. Even in love, even asleep. It looks so fair, Sometimes one of them will tear at it, but they can't take it off, can't, can't. Sometimes they reach inside and rend their own skin—most of them, at the last, did this. The face or the mask or both, with scratches, cuts, bruises. It rubs, *rubs*, like grit in the shoe that makes a sore. But this makes sores on the *soul*. I gained the knowledge from the Orichalci. I went through steel and thorns, biting ants, and fire and blood to gain it. I gained it whole and entire. Their shamans use such things only in great extremity. A clever people, who can call out the psyche in their ceremonies. A cruel people. Cruel as God. Do you see?"

"Yes."

"Before Carnival is over, those we select are eaten away as if a rat had been gnawing them. They kill themselves, or only die. For del Nero, that rival you love so well, it was his need of my daughter, or so he thought, that clawed and chewed him out. Only when he went under, when his lungs were full of green mud, did the mask fly up. And you found the mask, my dear. You found the mask that had killed him. And so came back to me like my little lost dog."

Furian stood by the black marble chair. He felt nothing. He had known, it seemed. The masks, what else. The masks were themselves the murderers.

"But one other small magic was in it," said Lepidus the wolf. "In a moment, I'll say. First, I insist you look at Calypso. Lunario had her. But so did I. What a pot of dolche she is. But that wasn't why we took her, not from affection, I regret. No one paid us to kill her. But she is to be killed, you see. This very night."

"Your explanations explain nothing. It only gets blacker."

"Yes, it does do that. You could have Calypso now. She'd be so willing. And luscious. And poor Eurydiche— so *mortally* jealous, watching *you* at work on another woman."

Furian felt Lepidus' burning hand fasten on him through his clothes. Lepidus fondled Furian just as he fondled his own self.

And Furian was hot as fire, cold as a grave, yet he twitched and filled to bursting, in the grip of his enemy.

Lepidus said, "Eurydiche is the focus for it all. I made her mine. She became the Venus mirror. I shine the light of sorcery on her and she reflects it back, on *them*. For this reason she has always met each one. With some she has been more than courteous. In Messalina's bed—she was there too. Did she like it, you ask again. Who knows. I told her she must."

"I don't follow you," said Furian. He did not bother to move away and Lepidus let him go.

"But you do follow. You're familiar with magic. What is Eurydiche but a symbol. And through the glass of her speechless void, through the abyss of all her screaming silence, *this* passes, and is magnified. Go down and take your pleasure with Calypso. Eurydiche will see. That will be enough, with *you*. The masks kill slowly, but this once, very fast. Take Calypso in the mask—it will finish her. Send her down to Juseppi in Avernus. He'll

FACES UNDER WATER

like that. She'll have to put him together as Isis did
Osiris."

"You do it," said Furian, "if it takes your fancy."

"But you were to be obedient. Obedient or dead
yourself. And you've killed quite often and easily. I tested
you twice, and saw you do it."

"Why? Why do you want me to—"

"To assume my mantle. I've done enough. Even the
masks have done enough. Calypso is to be the first, your
test. You'll kill those I choose, through Eurydiche and
through your own appetite. Better than a father, a *lover*."

"The masks kill—but you say, not without her. You
say that Eurydiche—that *she* kills them— "

"*She*." Lepidus stroked his penis. "I made her. I had
her. She never knew how I used her after. My lust, all
lust, caused such turmoil in her poor breast. And the turmoil must get out again—but how? She has no speech,
can't even blink. Such surging emotion will find an out-
let. If not through the lips or eyes, then through the
*heart*. Each sun of pain or fear, even the fear of an
unwanted, demanding love, reflects into her glass. And
is sent off from her so fiercely it can start a fire. Did she
know it? No. How could she? She met these persons and
never even knew they died, living put away as she did.
But then—ah, Furian. You appeared. With you, she's
different. With you, came love and healing, and her mirror turned to coolest, purest ice. So you see, there must
be made more strife. Terror again, and agony. Out of
such bliss, twisted, can emerge a scythe worthy of the
Angel of Death itself. She'll only need to see you put
your hands on Calypso. And you'll have your revenge,
on my daughter, for all this quagmire into which, unwit-
tingly, she dragged you; She knows now what she is and
has been. I told her she was a murderess, that same

night, yesterday, when I walked into the room and showed her that I still lived. and told her so did you. She knows how I've employed her, the lure and the weapon, both. Not only her use in their beds, their *gravemaker*. When you met her in that little room, did you find her more strange? Did you wonder why she had no paper and pen to write to you? You abhor her and you love her. Go down and straddle the red sow. And Eurydiche will weep and shriek behind her living mask. And Calypso's peppery brain will explode. This, my Furian, your final initiation into my service. This, or your death. Choose."

Furian turned. He looked at Lepidus. The thick body was bloated with its feeding. On the stroked rod, a pearl of excitement had broken out. Furian breathed, and even at this intake of air, fragments of rotten, sizzling power sprang to protect the monster, round its chair. Furian put one finger to them, and was burnt.

Furian lowered his eyes. "I've chosen. Kill me."

Lepidus rocked with some sudden turbulence. The mask only snarled.

"Are you sure? Sure? It was my best wish, to hear you ask for death. Even better than ruling your life, wearing you away."

"Then get on with it."

And now Furian shut his eyes, and put out the fires, the figures, the black room, all the magic, the chaos.

Something seized him. It was like the pressure of twenty nailed hands. He was swung up and up. Vertigo forced him to open his eyes once more. He hung in the boiling ceiling among worms of scalding gold. There was ice and flame together there, but he was stretched head downwards. He could not move. He heard the drum, and felt the horror of utter darkness, and of white light, of cessation and eternity. And waited for one ultimate blow.

ALL THE GODS WERE TAKING exercise by lashing him with golden flails. His ankles were held in manacles of gold that were not real, yet were stronger than iron.

He swung a little at each lash, but none of these were the final blow.

His head was full of blood and in his ears the drums pounded.

Below, perhaps only thirty feet from him, he saw the little figures. He did not worry about them. He wished to be dead.

But Furian's brain, his mind—not his soul—seemed loosened from his body. He moved away from the self hung there like a dead hare in the Butchers Quarter. He saw, without eyes, more clearly.

Lepidus had got up from his black throne, though the other three beast-men sat as they were, to North and South and West. He was coming down the steps, his member standing out ahead of him. He went past Eurydiche, and, as if she could not help herself, she turned her head to watch.

(He might have lied once more. There was no proof she had not known. She might revel in all of it, the foreplay and the death.)

Lepidus walked slowly towards Calypso, weighed down by his indicating lust. He fancied, and would see to it himself. And Calypso, her head darting up and down and about like a bird's, awaited him, her hands already alighted on her breasts and holding them up like ripe fruit for his attention.

But Shaachen was busy at something too. He had

gone scampering forward. He caught hold of Eurydiche. He turned her about, with one hand, to look at him. Furian heard Shaachen's voice, "Come here, come here." He was drawing her to the middle of the chamber. Shaachen pointed up. Up to Furian's body hung from the dome. "Look. Who's that? You see. Look at him. He'll die like that. Handfast, unable to breathe. The blood to the brain bursts it." (Furian thought, vaguely, *Oh, only that then.*)

Eurydiche's head was raised, tilted back on her white throat. The veil came undone and drifted to her feet. Her face, its eyes. Even now, hung here or separated from himself, he wanted to kiss that upturned, pliant, lifeless, singing mouth. Her eyes were so brilliant, as if with tears. But her tears were locked inside.

Shaachen had got something out of his coat. He looked so exactly a rabbit, hopping about Eurydiche, scattering bits untidily on the obsidian floor. Where they landed, spread little puffs of luminescence.

The funny scratchy rabbit voice was mumbling.

These were the pieces of the ruined letter, the dried mush from his pocket. No one had bothered with them. But they must be magical still. Shaachen had formed a circle about them both, the girl and himself. He took her arms and said, "By almighty God, don't move. You must stay still." Her face went down and she looked at him. And in that instant the shark-masked man stood up and shouted in Lunario's voice.

The words were something arcane. A gust of power not light, not motion—streamed across the room and hit the paper circle. At once a snow-white, transparent globe swam up and covered Shaachen over and covered over Eurydiche.

"Lepidus!" Lunario thundered.

The other Guild men had also risen. (One, the bat faced man, had an erection too now, perhaps not from desire but startlement.)

Lepidus' wolf-face looked over its shoulder. He paused, his penis still nosing at Calypso's scarlet skirt.

"Why, Doctor. You're inventive after all."

Shaachen did not answer. He called in a high child-ish voice, "Come *now*, darling!"

Furian, out of his strangling body, and still in it, felt a sharp light smack to his cheek—a wing. He saw a black and white fluttering, sprung through one of the eyelets in the dome, now dive towards the floor.

It was the magpie. It swooped to Shaachen's shoul-der, strutted there half a second, and jumped free. As its black feet touched the circle of damp paper, the magpie altered.

Rising up, it *rose*. The occult bird of Virgo. It grew like a black tree dashed with white, up on the black legs like inky coral, up past Shaachen and the girl, up above them, until its black-hooked head stood the height of a tall man higher than they. It spread its wings of coal, and from its back shimmered the rich, the alien blue. The scissors of its beak opened. It cawed once, and the chamber groaned.

The shark, the bat, the bear, stood by their seats. Lepidus stood with his hand upon the breast of Calypso.

Shaachen took hold of Eurydiche, viciously now. He shook her a little.

"Furian will die. Your father will make that happen. Do you want it?"

She was only stone, and then the wind blew her back into a stem. The flower head tipped side to side.

"No? *No?* Be sure."

Quickly now she shook her head. The diamond

shrilled on her forehead. The coronet fell from her hair and spun away to the paper circle's edge, with a lick of fire.

"I can do as *he* does," said Shaachen. "I can use you as my mirror. But I'll kill your father instead." She was motionless inside Shaachen's hands. Shaachen said, skittish, "He spoke to me about my props. Don't need them if I have you. But it will take all of me, and more of Eurydiche. It will kill you outright. But Furian will live. Do you hear me? *He* does. Furian hears every word. Lepidus or Furian. And if it's Furian, then be positive, your death. What do you say?"

Her head fell back. Furian saw again into her face. She was expressionless for a cruel God had made her so. And yet he read it all, the tempest within her, the racing tide.

Furian's body roared for her— "*No!*"

But the head of Eurydiche was lowered, went up, then down. She had nodded.

Lepidus let go of his victim, wolf's head fully turning and out of its eyes his own, looking like two snakes.

But Shaachen was gobbling, gabbling, and showers of light and flame shot up and up. The magpie fanned its giant wings.

Furian struggled. He struggled to fall and break himself and all this.

There was a noise like shrieking. A thousand voices of the damned were in it. It split the drums of the ears. At the outer circle of the room, the brazen redness of the Orichalcian magic bubbled.

Furian could not help but see. Tossing in the sorcerous chains, he must behold her, the woman he had loved, standing beyond Shaachen's squeaky ranting, changing, changing into crystal. He could see through her now, as through the thinnest pane of glass.

A sapphire ignition where her eyes had been flared downwards and up. And suddenly, out of her glassy nothingness there shot four bolts of the coldest and most unearthly blue. To three of the four Cardinal points they ran, to shark, to bat, to bear, straight as arrows. And to a fourth point where a red wolf balanced on the hind legs of a man, one dazzling ray hurled like a spear.

The air sizzled and shattered. Its red periphery went almost to black.

Furian felt himself turning in the height of the ceiling, then dropping, slow as a feather, through a welter of nauseous lightnings. He hit the floor softly, and curled on his belly.

From here he saw that the mask of the shark had come alive, come alive and turned inward. Lunario was screaming, fighting with it. Blood fountained out from under the blue grey head, which with its ivory teeth, was tearing off his face.

Three others screamed as he did. The bats were free, feeding voraciously upon the man who had fallen, ripping at his face and eyes. The white bear was twisting off the entire head, and next, through the pandemonium, the crack of a man's neck bone was piercingly audible.

Lepidus, on his knees, wrestled howling and retching with the mask of the red wolf which tore out his throat.

"Stay where you are," said Shaachen, miles away. "Don't touch the circle. Be quiet."

"Eurydiche," he said.

"Silence," said the magician, in the voice of God.

Furian put his head on his arms and said no more.

When all the screaming ended, the beasts of the four masks flowed off from the wreckage they had made;

they fluttered and rolled down the steps and met together on the obsidian floor. And here they tore in turn each other apart, fur and wings and skin and pelt, eyes and teeth, and as they rent and twined and sundered, they melted down like lead in a fire, but not to gold, only to a filthy clinker, which finally, mercifully, was without life.

FURIAN ASSISTED CALYPSO to sit up. She had gone down not far from the bloody mess of Lepidus. Her gown was wetly splashed, but it did not show.

"Let me alone," she said. "Get away."

"Yes, but first this comes off."

He eased at her mask. The fastenings were complicated. She had knotted ribbons in under her hair, to be sure.

"No—no, don't. I'll die."

"You'll die if you wear it."

"Take it off and my face will go with it."

Furian leaned and kissed the tops of her soft breasts. She moaned. He said, "Trust me, it won't."

When he pulled the mask away, she was pale and wasted.

In her autumn countenance, the lines had deepened. Her eyes were sick, yet lit now by two waking stars.

"Am I alive?"

"Alive."

He kissed her lips, and standing up, got her to her feet. Abruptly she put her refound face into her hands and wept. He heard in it the name of Juseppi. He left her, and walked slowly to Shaachen across the floor. The paper circle had burned up. It was charcoal. Shaachen was kicking it aside, while the magpie, only of usual size, sat clucking on his shoulder and letting go clotted streamers of clean green excrement.

"Birdshit, the gobs of God," commented Shaachen.

"Why did you use her?" said Furian. "But then, you don't mind the occasional death. It's science, isn't it."

"If I might save a life, I take the risk. To live is worth a risk. But this Mask Guild within a guild, to kill was the pastime. So I came to see to them, if I could."

Furian looked down. Across the circle, Eurydiche lay. Her hair had come loose, and spread like white silks in the sinking light, from which all redness had been bled. She was made of milk-white flesh, not glass. In her eyes the flames winked blue, as if her lashes fluttered as they never could. Ashes of white roses. Ashes of the moon.

He knelt beside her and brought her against him and held her. He stared into her face.

"She was willing to die for you," said Shaachen, "you can never forget it. Is this love?"

Yes, love. Insane and unspeakable and undeserved, and unbelieved, until too late.

"And so she's dead."

"Touch the neck. Do you know nothing?"

Furian put his finger against her throat. The pulse of Eurydiche was as faint as the beating of a moth. Even as he felt it, it stumbled, ceased, turning his bones to water. Then resumed, reluctantly. If she breathed, he could not see it.

"Dying then. She'll die."

Shaachen flapped his hands. He was as ever ruthless, experimental. "I may save her. You saw. I'm crafty."

"You can't. You blasted her apart. She'll die. She's dead. Even you can't bring her back from that."

"Don't look back into your past," said Shaachen. "You've lost what you cared for, so must lose everything?

Don't you know the story of the first Eurydiche? Her lover glanced back at her, though warned not to. They were coming up from the Underworld, no less, and she was yet half dead. She couldn't, that way, bear his eyes, and was driven down again. If he'd waited, the sunlight would have made her whole. Impatience. Men are fools."

Furian put his face into her silver hair. He thought, *And after you darkness.*

# The Heart

As THE WEEKS PASSED, the season faded into winter. Along the canal a wanderer now and then went up and down, sometimes a boat with vegetables and fruit, once a procession with priests and incense, bearing an image of the Virgin Maria, to bring the rain. The Carnival was gone, like a gaudy cloud, behind the pale lemon sun.

While she lay in the narrow bed, the girl, recapturing the ability to breathe and be, thought of her small life. It was a dream, and glided before her in a dream's fashion, sad and surreal. She remembered the first house, among the fields, the mountains far away with their salty snows. But her mother was a memory less actual than the pious nuns, who were callous to her, telling her always to thank God and Christ, although she did not know for what. This era ended in the blaze of glory, her father. Another house followed, comforts, pleasures, learning. Until the summer day the fire was turned upon her. The rape. How she had blamed herself. Her fault, his savagery, (although again, she did not know why.) And afterwards she was bereft, for now she could never love him any more.

Her life then, without love. It was filled presently by the panoplies of sex. How awful, this vast procession, colors and glitters, ways and means. Hollow, and worse, for now, here, there, for one second, some mirage of sweetness—never to be found. Mostly, let it be said, abjection, misery, and shame.

All the mystery of the City and the earth lay beyond her secretive house. She thought her father took her to these feasts and festivals of Carnival, to punish her, since she had brought him down. She knew he used her as a whore for others. Some were partial to her sort, her freakish looks. Returning, she was drained as a leaf hidden from the light. And from light, she hid herself.

She had no scope for other things. She read of other worlds she might not enter. What was crying like? This constant weightless passage of unliquid tears, the *phantoms* of water, through the caves of her heart?

For she was empty. She was not alive. She lived, moved, and was asleep. Always, always asleep. She knew no other state.

One night. One night at her father's bidding, present at a place of masks where she might wander, among the groves and lamps, a man approached her.

He too was masked—and yet

At once she knew him. As if she had known him since her childhood. As if he were her brother. He spoke to her beneath the sheltering trees.

"Who are you, Madama?"

She could not speak, of course. Yet her heart broke, at the wonder of his known and beautiful voice, into a stretching ache, a flowering hurt of smile. And he said, cool as her tears that never fell, "Keep smiling." As if he knew it all.

From that moment, even as he left her, she became a part of him. And when at last she saw his face—mad from fever and anger, white and stripped of everything but nothingness, it was yet the face of the lover she had always had within her. Her own face, only made other, made male, made *human*. Made divine. The guardian angel vowed to her by God.

Nevertheless, within her sphere, Lepidus remained a power. It was he who had told her so much of Furian, explained that Furian, if with her, would be kept safe—although Lepidus had not said from whom or from what—*himself*. So she gave Furian over to Lepidus. And at the first, (lying) death of Lepidus, when all the temple—harsh and barren, the palace of some heartless god—crashed round her, adrift, she clung to Furian. Then lost him also, as she had dreaded she must, for in an earthquake nothing stands. As the lagoon closed over his head, too stunned to feel, she had known merely the sentence of desolation that is in the gift of every limitless desert.

Later, when Lepidus reappeared, reborn, and told her that Furian also lived, a terrified lightness dashed her up. And as she hung from these killing talons, Lepidus told her all the rest. What she had been constructed to be, his focus of murder, Nemesis. (This, the second rape.) In her newest hell, she did not blame herself, did not question. She wanted only the incredible miracle that had released her before, love—Furian—to cleanse her and repair her. As he had cleansed and repaired her of all injury and sexual taint. Furian alone could give her back what the heartless always take away—her heart. And when it seemed Furian, although he said he loved her, did not wish to love her, would not believe or accept her, she began to die. To which death, the death of her life before was a shining thing.

It was Shaachen who offered her real death in exchange for Furian's continuance. Paramount had been her wish to save her lover. But also it was her honor. She had been the cause of death; this then justice. But more than that. To die for Furian would prove to him forever what she could not otherwise display, that she loved him more than life. Even he could not argue with her death. He could not distrust her. Though he must remain alone, he must always know he had been *loved*.

The Jewish alchemist, in the winter days when he began to talk to her, told her firmly that he had promised her death because her sacrifice must be total in order that his magic work. She did not mind. She thanked him, writing in her fine controlled hand, for the opportunity he had given her of vindication. Not once did she inquire how she had been saved. what bizarre sorceries and medicines had brought it about. Nor how they had escaped from the Island of Smokes. She did not therefore know at first that Lepidus was no more on his pinnacle. How the hirelings of the Guild, flying in fright from the sounds in the chapel, had given no trouble. Of the reeking fish boat. Of arms locked round her, of silent words pressed into her skin and hair. She did not even know she was in Shaachen's disreputable palace. She asked only one thing, she asked it every day. *Will I see Furian?*

"Not yet," said Shaachen. "Not until you are entirely alive. He doubts me. I won't let him near, till he can have no doubts."

Nor would he speak much of Furian. Only that Furian had written to his father, and been answered. Only that Furian had gone to this church or that, or to the Primo. That he had prayed.

*For what?* she asked.

"For you. For himself. For all the world."

At last Shaachen related to her that Lepidus was

dead. He did not describe the manner. She knew that it had been through her, and by her consent. When Shaachen seemed reticent, Eurydiche wrote, *My only father is Furian. He is my brother and my son. My other self. I need no one else.*

"One day he'll die," said Shaachen, moving from the reticent to the crass.

*Then so will I.*

"Not for a long time," said Shaachen, perhaps compassionate. "Not now for a long time."

Occasionally she saw the woman who had been on the Isle of the Dead. Unmasked she had a handsome face, which day by day took on a bloom. She wore fine gowns and grew sleek. Once this woman, called like Eurydiche by a Greek name, Calypso, put her hands on her hips and spoke at some length. She had the story to give she was a rich man's daughter who had wed for love and so lost everything but for a crumbling floor in some palace. Her husband had been too good for her and died. "Now I'm here," she added, bridging her tale obliquely. "You'll think I'm a harlot, living off an old man. Well, he's fair to my boy. And he may be elderly, Signore Shaachen, but he knows more of the bed than any young one."

This educated old man one morning showed Eurydiche a letter he had written, dedicated to no one. Perhaps Furian was to read it, or the Alchemist's Guild. Shaachen's hand-writing was crabbed, and the magpie had trodden on the paper, further muddling some passages.

Shaachen's gist was that the Orichalci tribe, The Enemy, had put Lepidus under their curse for his presumption in appropriating their magic, and his villainy in misusing it. This curse drove him on to make all his mistakes. To hazard his powers against the rogue force of Furian, and the colossal force of true love. While blinding him to the talents of one such as the canny and venturous Shaachen. So such curses worked, little in themselves, building from the flaws of character, the inner qualms, of those on whom they had been set. He might have taken a lesson from what he had done to Furian at eighteen. Lepidus had been played like an instrument and sent at last out of pitch

After she had read this—it took a while, there were long portions of self-congratulation—Shaachen stood her up.

She wore a dress of jasper velvet, and he fussed a moment with her sleeves, like an old servant woman. Then told her she was now alive, and might go into the other room and try the harpsichord he had put there for her.

The room was long and reverberant, and veiled with webs and dust, through which the inconstant winter sunlight ebbed or flamed. The harpsichord was old, unpainted with stained yellow keys, where lay a black feather sheened with blue.

She touched the feather, then sat down.

It was a song she tapped quietly from the instrument, but not the lover's song Cloudio del Nero had made for her, which now the faithless City had quite forgotten. This was a tune of her childhood, and in her head she heard the words she could not sing.

*If he is mine then he will come to me.*
*If he is mine, I will be his.*
*If I am his he will be mine.*

She heard his step, as once before, and as before, made out she had not.

He put his arms about her so tenderly, so unbelieving. He drew her up, and turning to him, she saw the face of her father, her brother, her lover, her son. Furian. Her other self.

"You are alive," he said. "You are. In God's name, you are."

He was empty as a shore from which the sea had gone, the emptiness that had been in her, so long, so long ago. But now, her eyes on his face, and as he looked at her, she saw the sea return, the waters of great oceans, and cover him with truth and light, with strength and happiness and life. And with eternal life.